ODD MAN RUSH

MICHAELA GREY
ARIEL BISHOP

For everyone who's found love outside of society's norms. And for Aaliya. Prank your father for me, since I'm not there to do it.

1

When Rune Hedaya walked into the Kingfishers' locker room, dread crawled inside Eli McKenna's chest and curled up there.

Practice hadn't started yet, everyone still busy getting their gear on, and the room was the usual raucous mess of stick tape and balled up socks being hurled around, chirps and rude comments and bragging blending seamlessly into white noise that Eli effortlessly filtered out. He focused on getting his own gear in place, buckling his pads on and keeping his breathing slow and even.

He was shrugging into his chest protector when William Caron, their head coach, had ushered the tall stranger inside, a hand on his shoulder. It was a measure of the respect Caron commanded that the room immediately quieted, although maybe they were just curious about the newcomer. He was strikingly handsome, dark brown hair shaved close to the sides of his head and left long on top, with olive skin and sharp eyes that surveyed the room.

"Boys, this is Rune Hedaya," Caron announced. "He comes from the Spirit. He's a d-man, and we're gonna try out some pairings today."

The captain was the first to greet him, because there was a reason he was captain. "Seth Williams," he said, holding out his hand.

Rune took it as others crowded around.

Eli breathed through his nose, in and out, not looking over. He stood, gave himself a once-over, and then bounced on his skates several times to make sure everything was settled and secure. When he glanced up, Rune was walking toward him.

"Hi," he said, hand out. "Rune. Defenseman."

Eli accepted the hand, hoping his hesitation hadn't shown. "Eli McKenna," he said. "Um. Goalie."

Rune's eyes creased with amusement. Up close, they were a striking blue-green. "Is *that* why all the gear?"

He had a faint accent, but Eli couldn't place it. It sharpened the corners of his words, made them crisp and clear. He was grinning, waiting for a response, and Eli just shrugged awkwardly.

"You know what they say about d-men," he said. "Can't read a clue to save their lives, let alone a play. I was just helping you out."

Rune's eyebrows shot up and he burst out laughing. "*Ouch*! Guess I'll just have to prove you wrong, huh?"

Eli found himself smiling back without meaning to, and he ducked his head, breaking eye contact. "Yeah, sure."

"Rune," Seth said, appearing at Rune's elbow. "Come meet Ilya and Josh. Couple of our d-men."

"Nice to meet you, Eli," Rune said. "See you out there."

He let himself be pulled away and Eli took another deep breath, rolling his shoulders and letting the tension flow from him on the exhale.

Daved was watching him when he turned for the door. Sympathy, visible only to Eli who knew him so well, glimmered in his eyes.

Don't, Eli warned him silently, and Daved just nodded and pulled the door open for him.

ON THE ICE, it was better. But then, it was always better on the ice. Here, between his pipes, he knew what was expected of him. *Stop the puck.* That's all he had to know. All the training, all the discipline, all the stretching and exercising—it all came down to that.

He shaved down his crease methodically, breathing loud inside his helmet, as the rest of the team, roughly half in gold jerseys and the other half in purple, spilled onto the ice and spun out into broad loops and circles, cheerfully calling abuse at each other. Eli let it wash over him, in it but not of it. He went through his warmup routine, counting each part off in his head, until Coach blew his whistle.

"Eli against Väinö," he said. "Eli, you're gold team. Vinyl, you're purple, obviously. Here are the pairings," he continued, holding up the whiteboard. "Gold with me, purple with Rob."

Rob, the assistant coach, raised his whiteboard and Eli scrutinized it. Rune had been paired with Josh. They were talking quietly off to the side, heads together. Eli didn't try to listen in. He read the rest of the lines and headed back to his crease.

The first few minutes were a burst of frenetic activity, the players all coming off a two day break and more than ready to get back into action. Eli stayed loose and ready in his crease, watching the play like a hawk.

Jay tried a sharp angle shot off him and Eli blockered it away with ease. It was scooped up by Rune and dumped into the far end. Eli watched as they gave chase. Rune was a good skater, fast and balanced, with an agility that belied his size. He crashed the scrum in the far corner and flipped the puck out to Josh, who sent it backward to Seth.

Ilya picked Seth's pocket before Seth could make a move toward goal, though, and then they were all heading back toward Eli, Ilya on a breakaway out in front. Eli floated forward to the edge of his crease, watching Ilya bear down on him. He knew Ilya well enough by now to know when he was going to make his move. He always dropped his right shoulder, *there*—Rune came out of nowhere just as Ilya fired, hurling himself to the ice in front of the puck.

It hit him in the bicep and Rune grunted and slid in a sprawl of long limbs through Eli's crease. Eli caught his arm, stopping his forward motion, as Ilya skidded to a halt in shock and the others caught up.

"Is *practice*," he said accusingly. "Coach is kill me if I hurt new d-man in very first practice! Why you so stupid?"

Rune grinned up at Eli, still flat on his back. "Thanks for catching me. You're not too bad at this goalie thing."

"Yeah well, you're a lot bigger than a puck," Eli said, pulling off his blocker and extending a hand. "Slower, too."

Rune laughed as he took his hand, grip firm, and let him pull him to his feet. "Are you always this mean?"

"I'm honest," Eli countered, but he couldn't fight the smile on his face.

"Whoa, did you just make Reaper smile?" Jay demanded.

Eli rolled his eyes. "I smile, Davo. If I don't smile at you, it's because you're not funny."

"Does that mean I *am*?" Rune asked.

"Jury's still out," Eli retorted.

Coach blew his whistle. Rune winked at Eli and skated away.

So it went for the rest of practice. Every time anyone with the puck got close to Eli, Rune was there first, breaking their shot, spoiling their aim, sometimes straight out slapping the puck off their stick. He was as fast as he was agile, not afraid to use his size but also careful not to make unnecessary contact.

"Why the fuck did the Spirit let you go?" Eli overheard Josh demand during a lull.

Rune shrugged easily, his reply inaudible.

After the first ten minutes or so, Coach switched it up, putting Rune with Ilya. Their chemistry was obvious from the beginning, working off each other's passes seamlessly. Rune shot Eli a blinding smile as he swept by him at high speed, gone before Eli could even smile back.

At least he's having fun, Eli thought, but something prickled under his skin at the thought of Rune and Ilya being friends. He shut that thought down before it could really form, turning his focus back to the practice. Daved was barreling down on him with the puck and Eli knew from experience just how hard he was to stop at that speed.

It wasn't that he didn't want Rune to have friends, Eli told himself in the shower. He didn't even *know* Rune, it was ridiculous to be concerning himself with Rune's hypothetical relationships.

Eli turned his face into the spray and closed his eyes.

He'd just found himself watching for Rune's brilliant smile, wanting it turned on him. Wanting Rune's attention, his focus. On him.

But he couldn't want that, he reminded himself, and turned the shower off.

He came out of the shower to find the room deserted. Not surprising—he'd taken awhile. He dropped his towel and stepped into his underwear, pulling them up over his hips.

"Why do they call you Reaper?"

Eli spun.

Rune was leaning against the door, ankles crossed, turning his phone over and over between long fingers. He raised an eyebrow when Eli didn't immediately answer.

"Oh, uh—" Eli struggled to marshal his thoughts, reaching for his pants. "It's stupid."

"Try me."

Eli zipped his pants and picked up his shirt. "Because I don't have a sense of humor and I'm lethal between the pipes."

"So you're the grim reaper. I like it." That bright smile spread across Rune's face, making Eli feel like he'd been punched in the gut. He covered by sitting to put his socks on, focusing hard on what he was doing.

"What—why are you still here?" he asked without looking up.

"Oh, group of guys wanted to take me out for lunch at some place called Savour?

They said it's the team's favorite restaurant. I thought I'd see if you wanted to come with us."

Bad idea bad idea bad idea.

Eli shook the thought away and stood to step into his shoes. Going out to eat once with his team and the new guy wouldn't hurt anything. There was nothing *to* hurt. Rune was just being friendly.

"Sure," he said, and Rune's smile widened until Eli couldn't breathe.

"Awesome! Well, I don't have a car, so… any chance of a ride?"

Eli had the sinking sensation that he'd bitten off more than he could chew. He was helpless to do more than nod and grab his keys off the shelf.

Rune followed him out of the rink, keeping pace easily. He looked around, taking in the rain-soaked pavement and the trees that crowded above them, forming a lacy, green-shaded cover over their walk to Eli's car.

"Sure is pretty out here," he remarked.

"Could be worse," Eli allowed. "Could be east coast."

"Hey, east coast is gorgeous—oh, you're teasing me. Who says you don't have a sense of humor?"

Eli shrugged, unlocking the car. "People who think fart jokes are funny."

"Ah," Rune said, sliding into the passenger seat. "Jay."

"Among others."

The car fired up smoothly and Eli rubbed the leather steering wheel with one thumb. "So why *did* you get traded?" he asked as he left the parking lot. "If you don't mind saying."

Rune stretched his long legs out as far as they would go, lacing his hands over his belly. "That's classified," he said comfortably.

Eli felt the flush all the way up to his ears. "Right. Never mind."

"Oh hey, no!" Rune said, sitting up. "That was a joke, I'm sorry. A stupid joke. Not funny."

The flush burned hotter. Eli hunched his shoulders, clutching the wheel tighter, and said nothing. Now Rune would see exactly how humorless he was.

The pause was awkward and Eli didn't know how to fill it.

"I, uh… I didn't fit in with the Spirit, I guess," Rune said suddenly. He scratched his nose. "I didn't like how they relied on muscle and heavy hits to get the job done. They wanted me to be more aggressive. I just wanted to play. They wanted me to take players out, really hurt them. It didn't—it wasn't right."

Silence fell in the car as a pop singer crooned on the radio.

"My first year in juniors," Eli said after a minute, "my coach made me loosen one of my pipes. If anyone bumped into it, it would pop off immediately and I'd get a whistle."

"Oh," Rune said. "That's…."

"Yeah." Eli took a slow breath. "Dirty. Or at least weighting the game in our favor. It made me—it made me sick. I didn't want to cheat to get a win. If I didn't win clean, what was the point?"

"Yeah," Rune said softly. "I'm sorry."

Eli shrugged, turning the corner toward the restaurant and looking for a parking space. "It's over and I survived. So did you."

"Will they let me play hockey here?" Rune asked, and for the first time he didn't sound confident.

Eli parked and took a moment to gather his thoughts. "I think so," he finally said. "Cary—Coach—he may want you to hit someone sometimes, shake 'em up and put a little fear of God and the Kingfishers into them, but he'll have already seen your talent. You're not just big dumb muscle to him."

Rune was watching him when Eli looked at him. "You like him."

"And respect him," Eli said. "He's a great

guy. He'd open a vein for us and every single one of us would do the same for him. You'll see."

Rune's eyebrow went up. "Damn. So what do you like to do for fun?"

Eli blinked at the sudden shift in topic. "I mean, normal stuff," he hedged. "Why?"

"Just curious. You're so quiet. I wanna know what makes you tick."

"We should go inside," Eli said abruptly, and unbuckled.

Rune didn't move, watching him with narrowed eyes. "You like to drink? Party?"

"No," Eli said, startled into truth. "I'm boring. I like to read. I don't go out unless the team drags me out." He fidgeted with the seatbelt. "Why do you *care*?"

"Why do you think?" Rune asked cryptically. He pushed his door open and stepped out before Eli could answer, leaving him to swear and scramble after him.

The guys were already in the back of the restaurant at their favorite booth when they showed up, and they were greeted with cheers and chirping over being late.

They settled in, Rune right next to Eli on the bench, and Eli picked up his menu, determined not to notice how solid and warm Rune's thigh was pressed up against his own. He almost managed it until Rune nudged him with his knee.

"What's good here?" he asked under the chatter of the table.

Eli forced himself to focus. "The beef au jus is nice. Or they have an Italian sub that's not too far off our diet plan, especially if you get it with all the vegetables."

Rune smiled at him and when the server came by, he ordered the beef au jus. "So," he said once she was gone. "What's there to do around here, boys?"

"Webber will show you all the best coffeeshops," Jay said. "'Specially the ones with cute baristas. You got a girl, Runer?"

"No girl," Rune said equably, leaning back against the seat and spreading his arms along the spine. His fingers brushed Eli's shoulder and Eli forced himself not to react. "No guy, either."

The booth went momentarily still.

"That gonna be a problem?" Rune said. His voice was utterly calm.

"We see you play, you fuck anyone you want," Ilya said into the fraught silence. "You're not hit on me though. I have girlfriend. Very beautiful. You want see?" He was digging out his phone before anyone could stop him, thumbing through pictures and then holding it out so Rune could see.

"She *is* beautiful," Rune agreed. "What's she doing with your ugly ass?"

Ilya cackled. "NHL player, baby. Lots of money!"

Eli focused on the air entering his lungs, trapping it there, then letting it out slowly. Rune wasn't straight. Rune had been—possibly, unless Eli's wishful thinking had clouded his vision—hitting on him.

Rune's fingers brushed his shoulder again and Eli turned to look at him. Up close, Rune's smile was somehow even more beautiful, his striking eyes crinkling at the corners.

"We good?" he murmured under whatever Ilya was saying.

Eli took a breath. Another one. Rune waited.

"Yeah," Eli said. He mustered a smile, even though it wasn't very big. "Of course. So where are you from, anyway? I can't quite place your accent."

"Germany by way of Syria," Rune said. "My parents wanted a better life for their kids. Papa's an engineer and Mama's a doctor. Hey." He leaned closer and lowered his voice. "Do you wanna maybe hang out later? Just the two of us?"

Eli froze. Was he asking what Eli *thought* he was asking? The look in Rune's eyes said maybe, just maybe, he was.

He opened his mouth to say something

and his phone rang, cutting off his answer. *Shit.*

"Sorry," he muttered, dragging it from his pocket. "I have to get this."

"Is that Noemi?" Jay demanded, and Daved elbowed him in the ribs. "Ow! Tell her I said hi, Reaper. *Ow*, Davvy, stop it!"

"Who's Noemi?" Rune asked.

"Um." Eli slid from the booth, the phone still ringing. He glanced at Rune, looking up at him with nothing but friendly curiosity in his eyes, and back down at the phone. "My wife. Excuse me."

2

So that was that. The hottest guy Rune had ever seen and he was not only probably straight but very definitely married.

He took a deep swallow of his drink and forced himself to focus on the conversation.

Ilya was telling a story that apparently required a lot of hand waving. Rune nodded in the right places and very determinedly didn't look in Eli's direction. He was standing by the entrance, back to the table and shoulders hunched as he talked. To his *wife*.

It wasn't fucking fair. Rune had been positive he wasn't misreading the shy interest in Eli's eyes, the way he'd angled toward him even when he wouldn't or couldn't meet his eyes. The thought of coaxing him out of his shell, bringing that lovely smile to life, had been intoxicating.

It would be easier if he weren't so goddamn attractive, he thought sourly, slumping in his seat and stirring his drink with the straw. Eli wasn't tall or broad, but he was all sleek muscle and sturdy lines. Pale skin and fair hair Rune itched to touch fell into his face, over almond-shaped eyes the most stunning shade of clear gray Rune had ever seen.

Rune glanced up to see Daved studying him. Daved was dark, quiet, and intense, a thoughtful air to him. And currently he was inspecting Rune like he was a dissection project, his brown eyes sharp.

Rune raised an eyebrow and Daved just shook his head, as if that explained anything.

"So how do you like it here?" Jay asked, leaning forward to catch Rune's attention.

"I've been here for less than a day," Rune pointed out. "But it's nice. Very green. Does it ever get cold enough to snow?"

"Not really," Seth said. "But the forests make up for it. We go hiking a lot—good for team-building."

Eli returned to the table just then, slipping in beside Rune but not quite touching him. "Sorry," he said in that quiet, husky voice that had captured Rune's focus from the first moment he spoke. "Did I miss anything?"

"How's Noemi?" Jay asked.

"She's fine," Eli said, tone unreadable.

"Did you tell her I said hi?"

Eli fixed Jay with a look. "You do realize you don't have a chance with her, right?"

Jay blushed bright red. "That's not—I didn't mean—" He broke off as Eli huffed an almost-laugh.

"She says hi and wanted me to remind you to drink your milk."

Laughter went up around the table and Jay somehow blushed even harder, slumping in his seat.

"I'm not *that* much younger than her," he complained, but no one was listening.

"Rune," Seth said, cutting through the chirping. "Do you have a place to stay yet?"

Rune shook his head. "I was just gonna get a hotel and figure it out later."

"Oh no," Seth said. "We're not having our new star d-man in a hotel. The team usually has an apartment but the pipes burst and it's being renovated, so you'll come home with one of us. Who's got room?"

"He can crash on our couch," Jay offered.

Seth snorted. "I've sat on that couch. We want him able to play. I'd take him but Marissa would kill me if I don't at least give her a chance to clean out the guest room."

"It's fine, really—" Rune began.

"Hey, Eli's got a spare room!" Jay interrupted.

Rune hid the cringe. *Really,* really *bad idea, kid.* But before he could think of an excuse, Eli had nodded.

"I'll need to check with Nome, but of course you can stay with us, Rune." He pulled out his phone and began texting as Rune stewed silently.

Staying with Eli? This was going to be a disaster. His traitorous brain supplied him with images of Eli in the morning, sleep-rumpled and soft, or coming out of the bathroom in nothing but a towel, and Rune opened his mouth to tell him he'd be fine, this really wasn't necessary.

"She says of course," Eli said before he could speak. "And she wants to know if you have any allergies or food dislikes."

"No allergies, I'll eat anything," Rune said, his heart sinking. It was too late to get out of it. *It's fine,* he told himself sternly. *Grow up. You read him wrong, he's taken and not interested and this is a friendly offer between teammates.* God, he needed to get laid. Maybe he could do that once he'd settled in.

Eli smiled at him, nothing but friendliness on his face. "You have your bag with you?"

"Yeah, the rest of it will be shipped up once I have an address."

"Perfect. You'll just come home with me, then."

Seth clapped once. "That's settled."

"You'll love Noemi," Jay told Rune earnestly.

Not fucking likely. Rune summoned a smile. "She had the good taste to marry this stud," he said, bumping Eli's elbow. "I'm sure I will."

Eli coughed, ears going dull red, and developed a fascination with his drink.

Noemi

Noemi tucked her phone into her pocket and did her best not to panic.

She knew, better than most of the team's significant others, what it was like to have a partner who was a professional athlete, the weird, quasi-familial bond that made a good team. She'd grown up with players and rookies around even before Adam had started getting serious about hockey.

So when her husband texted asking if the new d-man could stay in their spare room for a week or two instead of a hotel, she knew what the answer had to be. Just like Eli had known before he sent the text.

Taking a breath, she held it and then exhaled as slowly as possible. At least she'd gotten off early today, and since Eli and the new guy were out with the team, she had a little time.

There was no telling what kind of a person this Rune was, and how he'd react if he learned he was sleeping in what was pretty clearly Noemi's own bedroom, not a spare. Not that there was anything wrong with couples, even happily married ones, having separate bedrooms.

But it still wasn't a question she wanted to answer. Squaring her shoulders, she headed for her room, making a mental list of the stuff she'd have to remove so the room looked unlived in. The situation was what it was, and it was up to her to make the best of it.

She always did.

Rune

Eli and Noemi lived not far from the practice rink, in a nice but not ostentatious neighborhood. The house was a squat bungalow, with a wide front porch and a cobblestone path leading up to it.

Rune shouldered his bag and followed Eli to the door.

"I'm home!" Eli called.

Something fell and shattered, and a woman shrieked.

"I'm going to *murder* you!" she screamed from the back of the house, and the sound of running feet echoed through the hall where Eli and Rune stood frozen, staring at each other. "Just wait until your father gets home, just *wait*, you little *shit*—"

A sandy-colored dog barreled around the corner and launched itself at Eli, who knelt to greet it.

"What'd you do?" Eli asked, rubbing the dog's ears. "What'd you *do*, bud?"

The dog wriggled and licked his hands, wagging its tail frantically, as more footsteps sounded and a small, curvy woman appeared. She had dark hair, blue eyes snapping with fury, and flour coating her front, from her shoulders to her toes.

Eli looked up and his eyebrows climbed. "Oh."

"Yeah," Noemi said. "*Oh*. We're having filet of dog for dinner."

Eli didn't bother stifling his laugh as he stood. "Noemi, this is Rune. Rune, this is—um, my wife. Noemi."

Noemi held out a hand, then yanked it back and shook the flour off it, glaring at the dog. "Hi, Rune," she said sourly. "It's *great* to have you here, what a wonderful first impression this is, welcome to our home. Don't go in the kitchen, there's broken pottery on the floor."

Rune pressed his lips together tightly to keep from smiling. "Hi," he said. "Thank you for having me."

"And this is Archer, but don't get attached," Noemi continued, glaring at the dog, who wagged his tail even harder. "He's not going to be here long."

Rune bent to greet the dog, conflict pulling at him. Noemi was not only lovely —Rune was gay, not blind—but also charming and apparently funny. But of course she was. He already knew Eli wouldn't have married a boring person.

Archer wriggled happily as Rune rubbed his ears. When he straightened, Eli had an arm around Noemi's shoulders and she was smiling up at him. Rune's stomach sank. This was going to suck.

"Are you hungry, Rune?" Noemi asked. "Assuming my husband's horrible hound will stay out of my way, dinner should be ready in about half an hour."

"He's only a little bit hound," Eli pointed out. "Mostly lab."

Noemi glared at him, ducked out from under his arm, and marched back down the hall. "Show Rune where he'll be staying," she tossed over her shoulder. "And then come help me cook."

Eli took Rune down the hall past a spacious living room. He opened a door at the end of the passage and held it as Rune stepped inside, glancing around curiously.

It was a nice room. The walls were painted a soft yellow, glowing in the afternoon sun and casting a golden tint on the hardwood floors. Another door on the far side of the room stood open, a sink and part of a shower visible from where Rune stood. The bed wasn't huge, but it looked comfortable, covered in a quilt that looked handmade, a riot of green and yellow and brown.

"It's great," Rune said, setting his bag down. "You really didn't have to do this, you know."

Eli shrugged, still standing in the doorway. "I don't mind. But we're not exciting people."

Rune tilted his head. "What exactly do you think of me? That I'm some relentless party animal?"

"No!" A flush crawled up Eli's throat again. "I'm not—I didn't mean to imply anything. It's just… you're…. Forget it."

"I'm what?"

Eli rubbed the back of his neck. "You're just… really cool," he muttered. "With your designer sneakers and expensive jeans and that haircut, I thought—"

Amusement trickled through the tangled knot of emotions in Rune's chest. "You think I'm cool?"

Eli glowered. "I think you look like *you* think you're cool."

"Nah," Rune said, grinning. "You just said I'm really cool."

"I definitely did not," Eli snapped. "Bathroom's through there." With that, he spun and stomped out.

Rune laughed quietly to himself. He sat down on the bed, leaning back on his hands, and gazed around the room. Part of him wished it wasn't so welcoming. He didn't *want* to like it there, any more than he wanted to like Noemi. But at least he'd be comfortable until he found a place of his own, which was going to be top of his to-do list.

He unpacked his bag and then went in search of Eli. He found him in the kitchen, helping Noemi sweep up flour and pottery shards.

"What actually happened?" Rune asked.

Noemi blew a dark strand of hair out of her eyes and held the trash bag open for Eli to dump the flour into. "I was trying to make a roux. Archer got under my feet just as I picked up the container, and—" She gestured. She'd changed while Rune was gone, into a sleeveless shirt the color of mulberries that made her skin glow and a pair of black capris.

"Can I help with anything?" Rune asked.

Noemi smiled at him, a dimple flashing in her cheek. "Can you make a salad?"

"Sure."

Eli slipped by Rune in the doorway with a murmured "excuse me". Rune carefully didn't watch him leave. Instead he went to wash his hands in the sink and then stationed himself at the counter Noemi indicated. He chopped walnuts and tore lettuce as Noemi worked at the stove, muttering under her breath. Archer was in a doggy bed in the corner of the sunny kitchen, watching the proceedings with interest but not moving.

"So, Rune," Noemi said. "Tell me about yourself. How long have you been playing hockey? Do you have a specific team you dream of playing with? Any family nearby? Significant others?"

"One at a time, Nomes," Eli said mildly,

reappearing in the doorway. He washed his hands and dropped a kiss on the cheek she offered up as Rune stared at the walnuts.

"Um. I'm German, but my parents emigrated from Syria before I was born. I have an older brother and a younger sister."

"Are they into hockey?" Noemi asked, resting a hip against the countertop to watch him.

"Well, they follow it because of me, but they're not involved professionally." Rune scooped the chopped walnuts into a bowl and turned his attention to the pears. "My sister's an accountant and my brother works for the government."

"They're all still in Germany?"

Eli pulled a beer from the fridge and held it up to Rune in silent question. Rune nodded and Eli popped the lid and set it on the counter beside him before turning to the vegetable peeler and waiting potatoes.

"They come for important games. They were here for the playoffs last year."

"That was a good run," Eli offered.

"Not good enough," Rune said. He kept dicing the pears, not looking up. "What about you, Noemi, what do you do? Er… do you work?"

Noemi snorted. "Of course I work. I'm the assistant coach for Seattle U's men's hockey team."

"Oh," Rune said. "Oh wow, that's amazing. Do you like it?"

"Fucking love it," Noemi said cheerfully. She pulled out a loaf of bread and set to slicing it. "People can be assholes, but I've been there long enough that they mostly take me seriously now. Being married and my pedigree helps, although I don't advertise it."

"Your... pedigree."

Eli cleared his throat. He looked oddly abashed. "I, uh... didn't get a chance to tell you, earlier, but Noemi's father is. Um. Our coach."

Rune stared at him. "You're William Caron's son-in-law."

Eli attempted a smile. "Guilty?"

Noemi sighed loudly. "Seriously, E, you've gotta start actually telling people you're related to him."

"But it sounds like name-dropping," Eli protested. "Or bragging, or... I don't know. What if people think it's nepotism?"

Noemi rolled her eyes, inviting Rune to join her. Rune gave her a weak smile, his mind spinning. William Caron's *son-in-law*. It wasn't surprising Eli wanted to keep it secret—people could be shitty, Rune knew all too well.

"If anything, he's harder on you than everyone else," Noemi pointed out. "He doesn't want people to think favoritism any more than you do."

"So that's how you guys met?" Rune scooped blue cheese from the container and sprinkled the crumbles over the salad. "How long have you known each other?"

Noemi gave Eli a soft smile. "Three years now. He came in on a one year contract but he fits so well he signed a five year one when it was up."

"Did you know right away, when you saw each other?" Rune asked. He wasn't sure why he was pushing. *Small talk*, he told himself, but that wasn't it. He was at least honest enough to admit that. It was like pressing on a bruise, watching the way Noemi lit up as she detailed how she'd been delivering something to her father's office and literally run face-first into Eli, who'd been hurrying to practice.

"It wasn't love at first sight," Noemi said. She set the lid on the pot she'd been stirring and rounded the counter to lean against Eli's side. He pressed a quick kiss to her hair but didn't stop peeling potatoes. "But we hit it off. We had so much fun. We were finishing each other's sentences by the end of the first hour we spent together."

Eli was looking at the potatoes like they held the secrets to the universe. After a minute, Noemi stirred and went to the fridge for a beer of her own.

"Anyway, friends turned into best friends turned into… this." She gave Rune a brilliant smile. "We figured, we spend all our time together anyway, we might as well make it official."

"That's beautiful," Rune said. He turned away to wash the blue cheese off his hands, fighting to keep his expression neutral. When he turned back, he was smiling.

"What about you?" Noemi asked. "Anyone important in your life?"

"Ah, no," Rune said. He hesitated briefly and Eli looked up, catching his eye. He nodded briefly, and somehow Rune got it. Noemi was safe. He could tell her. "I'm—I guess you could say I'm open to the possibility, but I'm not actively looking right now. If he walks into my life, that'll be great. If not, I've got plenty to keep me busy."

Noemi's eyebrows arched, but all she did was smile. "Seattle has a great gay scene. I used to work at this really fabulous gay bar when I was in college—I'll give you the name if you want. Very discreet, wonderful people."

"Once I'm settled in," Rune said, smiling back in spite of himself. "I'd love to have it."

3

Eli

"I like him," Noemi said with her toothbrush in her mouth.

Eli hummed noncommittally, turning the page of his book.

"He's sweet," Noemi continued. "And Archer likes him, so obviously he's a decent guy."

Eli snorted. "You can't let our *dog* decide who's on the approved list. He hates the mailman, remember?"

"I've always thought that mailman was shady," Noemi said darkly, appearing from the bathroom in a lacy nightgown that bared her thighs. "He's hiding something, I can *feel* it."

Eli pulled the covers on her side down. "He's a perfectly nice guy. He even hides our packages when we're not home so they don't get stolen. What's wrong with him?"

"He's shifty," Noemi said, sliding into the bed. "Anyway, we're off-topic. Do *you* like Rune?"

"Sure," Eli said. He cleared his throat, closing the book he'd been pretending to read and setting it on the nightstand.

"*And* he's super hot," Noemi continued. She scooted close and draped an arm over Eli's waist. "Like holy-shit-he-should-be-a-model hot. That hair. And those *eyes*. And you can tell he's absolutely jacked—"

"Nomes," Eli interrupted somewhat desperately. "We should probably sleep."

"*Is* he jacked?" Noemi asked. "You get to see him in the locker room, you lucky bastard. Come on, tell me everything."

"I am telling you *nothing*," Eli said, rolling over and presenting her with his back.

Noemi giggled—God, Eli loved her laugh—and slid across the bed to plaster herself against him. "I married you so you'd tell me all the gossip about your team," she said in his ear. "You have to hold up your end of the bargain, McKenna."

Eli reached back and found her arm, pulling it across his waist. "Hey," he said. "I should have asked you sooner, but—are you gonna be okay with him here?"

Noemi squeezed his waist and sat up. Eli rolled to look at her as she crossed her legs, looking sober.

"We're not talking years, right?" she said, rubbing his forearm with a thumb. "I'll be fine."

"But if you—"

"I'll be fine," Noemi repeated, tone suddenly sharp, and Eli flinched. Contrition flashed across her face and she wrapped cool fingers around his wrist. "I'm sorry, babe. I just—it's stupid. I shouldn't need… I'm *married* now. I belong here, with you."

Eli sat up, mirroring her pose, and took her hands. "Do you have any idea how many couples sleep separately?"

"Happily married ones?" Noemi shot back.

"Yes," Eli said immediately. "Sometimes one of them snores. Or kicks. Or sometimes, like you, they just need their own space. It's not—you're not avoiding me. You need alone time. You think I don't get that? I'm the world's biggest introvert, of course I understand you wanting your own bed."

Noemi chewed on her lower lip.

"What I'm worried about more is the fact that he's in your room," Eli said gently, watching her face. "I know you felt you had to say yes, but—"

"He's team," Noemi said. "And I like

him, I really do. He's quiet and doesn't get in the way, and I'm not gonna be the asshole making him get a hotel his first night in town."

"Still."

"It'll be fine," Noemi said, and kissed him. Her lips were soft and Eli closed his eyes and tried to kiss her back. "Sleep time," she said when she pulled away, and she was smiling at him.

"I love you a whole lot," Eli said helplessly.

"Well, who could blame you?" Noemi said.

IT DIDN'T TAKE her long to fall asleep—even when they shared a bed, it rarely did. It took Eli longer, alone with his thoughts and the guilt that tainted everything he touched, a slick miasma of self-hatred.

He never should have married Noemi. He knew that. But he'd been a coward, and weak, and craving something—*someone*—safe. Noemi was the eye in the hurricane of his life. She carried peace with her, a soothing mantle that calmed Eli just by being near her.

But he couldn't give her what she needed. They'd been married for three months and he could count on one hand how many times they'd had sex in that time. Not that she often initiated either—even when they'd first been dating, they'd fallen asleep watching movies far more than they'd fooled around.

Did she want more? It was impossible to know, with Noemi. She was one of the most even-tempered people he'd ever met. It was one of the things that had drawn him to her—her ability to keep an even keel when everything was falling apart around her. Eli's life rarely made sense, but when she was around, it did.

He just had to try harder, he thought. Noemi's breathing was slow and deep beside him. She deserved better. She deserved all of him, not just bits and pieces.

As for Rune… it would be fine. He wouldn't stay long in any case. Eli would make him feel welcome, keep his thoughts to himself, and soon enough he'd be gone and Eli and Noemi could get back to their lives.

He didn't feel any better, but he closed his eyes and did his best to fall asleep.

Rune found him in the kitchen the next morning, his hair damp from his shower.

He smiled at Eli, the early sun highlighting the planes and angles of his face, and Eli instinctively smiled back.

"Breakfast is almost ready," he said, and flipped the pancake.

"I like Noemi," Rune said, settling at the counter and pouring himself orange juice from the pitcher in front of him.

Eli stopped moving briefly. "I'm fairly fond of her too," he finally said, forcing his voice to stay light and even.

"She fits you," Rune continued.

Eli swung to face him, startled. "What does that mean?"

Rune shrugged. "I mean she… settles you. I don't know how to explain it. You're just less tense around her, I guess."

"I'm not tense," Eli protested, the lie stinging his throat.

Rune just raised an eyebrow. "You're wound about as tight as it's possible to be, bud."

"You don't know me," Eli snapped.

"But maybe I want to."

Eli shut his mouth abruptly. Rune was watching him over the rim of his glass, eyes intent.

"I'm—" *Married. Unavailable. Not out in any conceivable way, even to my own wife.*

"Friends, Eli," Rune said gently. "I want to be your friend. You think that's possible?"

Eli swallowed hard and turned to rescue the burning pancake. "I don't—Dav's my only real friend, besides Noemi," he said without looking. "I'm not saying no, but…." *You'll stop trying very quickly.*

"Morning!" Noemi chirped. She was wearing her running gear, silky brown hair pulled up in a ponytail. "Rune, how'd you sleep?" She pecked Eli on the cheek on her way past to the refrigerator and he leaned into it absently.

"Great," Rune said. "That bed is seriously comfortable. I slept like a rock."

"What do you guys have planned for today?"

Rune looked questioningly at Eli, who wracked his brain.

"Practice, then a media scrum to welcome Rune, Cary said. Then tonight we leave for our next road trip."

Knowing his luck, he'd be roommates with Rune on the road, Eli thought.

"Rune, you're rooming with Ilya," Caron announced after the media scrum.

Eli didn't look up from his seat in the corner, feet tucked beneath him. He was relieved, he told himself.

"I want you two to form a bond," Caron

continued. "I think you'll be a great d-pair if we can get that chemistry going. The rest of the team has been shuffled a bit as a result. Eli, you're with Daved. Jay, you're with Seth. That way he can sit on you when the hyper-activity hits."

"I'm nearly twenty years old!" Jay protested over the laughter.

"Yeah, in eleven months," Seth added, grinning.

"Go home and pack," Caron said, ignoring them both. "Plane leaves at five, be there at four."

ON THE PLANE, Eli settled into his usual seat, his teammates doing their usual chirping and jostling and shoving as they found their places.

A pair of feet appeared in his peripheral vision and Eli looked up to see Rune smiling at him.

"This seat taken?" He was sitting down before Eli could answer.

"Hey," Daved complained, a yard down the aisle.

Rune gave him a cheeky grin and Eli sank lower in his seat, staring at the in-flight magazine in the rack in front of him.

"Why are you here?" he asked quietly.

"Do you want me to go?" Rune put his hands on the armrests and Eli shook his head immediately.

"No, I—sorry. I don't… I just don't understand why you want to be my friend."

Rune looked briefly sad. "I'm making you uncomfortable. I just thought… we're going to be roommates for at least a couple of weeks, while I look for a place. I want you to feel comfortable with me and I can tell you don't. And I'd like to be your friend, I really would. But I didn't mean to push so hard. I'll leave you alone, okay?"

Eli grabbed his arm and Rune froze, half out of his seat. Eli let go just as fast, pulling back like he'd been burned, but Rune sank back to the cushion, staring at him.

"Don't go," Eli said. "I'm not good at… friends. But—I'd like to try?"

This is all wrong, he thought as the smile spread across Rune's face. He'd just promised himself he'd commit to Noemi and be there more fully for her, and now here he was actively seeking out friendship with a man he was deeply attracted to. Self-hatred threatened to choke him and he swallowed hard, forcing it back. *It's for Rune's sake*, he told himself, but he knew it was a lie.

"So what do you and Noemi do for fun?" Rune asked.

"We usually run together—there's a jogging trail behind the house. I'll show it to you when we get home if you want. But we're both pretty quiet. We mostly stay in, read. Sometimes go to the movies. Neither of us is big on lots of people."

"You sure you're okay with me being in your space?" Rune asked.

"I asked Nomes last night," Eli said abruptly. "If she meant it when she welcomed you to our home."

Rune raised an eyebrow.

"She likes you," Eli said. "I'll be honest —at first we *did* say yes because Jay volunteered us. Not an easy or graceful way to say no to that, you know?"

Rune grimaced. "Yeah. I'm sorry."

Eli waved that off. "Not your doing. But you fit in well. Archer likes you. You cooked with us, you didn't make any noise, you're a good guest. And—" He swallowed. "I like you."

Rune said nothing, but his eyes lit with a quiet joy.

"Don't get a big head," Eli warned him. "I'm just saying we're happy you're with us. For as long as you need."

He told himself Rune's smile affected him not at all.

Daved waited to talk to him until they were in the room, both dressed for bed and unwinding.

"So, Rune."

"No," Eli said immediately.

Daved looked unimpressed, stretched out on his bed with arms behind his head. "You like him."

"Dav, please—"

"I know," Daved said. "I *know*. I just… hate what you're doing to yourself."

Eli rubbed his face. Anyone else, he'd have already left the room, shut the conversation down wholesale, but this was Daved, his best friend through college, who'd been drafted by the Wolverines and then traded to the Kingfishers, who'd always been there for Eli no matter what.

"What does Noemi think of him?" Daved asked, his voice quietly neutral.

"She likes him," Eli said. He dropped his hands and sighed. "He likes her. He won't be with us for long, anyway. Just until he finds a place."

"She's okay with him being in her room?"

"I think she's not thrilled with the setup, but us being gone for three days will help in any case, give her time alone."

Daved nodded, looking thoughtful. "When are you gonna tell her, E?"

Eli's throat closed. "Never," he managed.

"You're going to lie to your best friend for the rest of your life?" Daved asked gently.

"I already did that," Eli spat. "I did that when I married her. If I tell her *now* that I didn't mean my vows, what does that make me?"

Daved sat up. "But you *did* mean your vows."

"No, I—"

"I was there, remember? You promised to love and honor her, to be by her side for the rest of her life, to support her in whatever she chooses to do. I didn't hear anything in your vows about promising to be sexually attracted to her."

Eli wrapped his arms around his knees, pressing his face against them. "A lie by omission is still a lie."

Daved sighed. "Buddy, she sleeps in her own room. You told me she started doing that right after the honeymoon. How often do you guys have sex?"

"Maybe twice a month," Eli said. The shame threatened to drown him, and he kept his face down.

"And how often does she initiate?" Daved asked carefully. "Think about it honestly for me."

Eli closed his eyes, obeying unwillingly.

The last time had been nearly two weeks ago. They'd both been tipsy. Noemi had kissed him while they were laughing about something, and Eli had told himself she wanted more, so he'd deepened the kiss and rolled her on top of him.

The time before that, she'd been upset by a misogynistic comment from a coworker. Eli had kissed her to distract her, it had worked, and he'd gone with it.

And the time before—Eli opened his eyes.

"It's me," he said, voice rusty.

Daved lifted an eyebrow.

"I think she initiated a couple of times on the honeymoon, but we spent most of that week drunk anyway. It's—since we came home, it's pretty much always been me." He looked up. "What does that mean?"

"It means you need to talk to her," Daved said. "Does she ever turn you down?"

"I guess, yeah…." Eli thought back again. "Maybe once or twice since we've been married. A few more times before that when we were dating. Fuck." He scrubbed at his face. "Why is this so *complicated*?"

"People are messy as fuck," Daved said. "There's no binary option, much as some idiots will try and insist there is. There's no wrong way to love, E, as long as you're honest and open about it. But you're not being honest, are you?"

Eli closed his eyes again. "Fuck you."

Daved laughed, sympathy rich in the sound. "I know, buddy. I'm gonna sack out, okay? Try to get some sleep at some point. We need you on your game tomorrow night."

THE LIGHTS OFF and Daved's breathing slow and deep in the bed beside him, Eli texted Noemi.

We're at the hotel. Enjoying your time alone?

She responded immediately. *Watching TV w/Archer. He says this episode is badly written, but he licks his own butt, so what does he know.*

Eli laughed softly under his breath. He missed her like air when they were separated, the way she had of settling his nerves, reassuring him that everything really would be alright. He could imagine her curled up on the couch, feet tucked beneath her and Archer sprawled on top of her, the light from the television flickering on her beautiful face. His heart squeezed.

Miss you, he sent.

You too, she replied. *Kick ass tomorrow.*

I'm gonna hang out with Juliet after work but I'll watch the game.

He'd talk to her when they got home, Eli thought. Once he'd had a chance to put his thoughts in order.

4

Noemi

"How the fuck long has it been?" was the first thing out of Juliet's mouth when Noemi walked into the restaurant, followed by, "and why the fuck is it always me calling you, bitch?"

Noemi laughed and hugged her. Juliet was easily six inches taller than her, her olive skin gleaming and messy pixie cut throwing her perfect cheekbones into relief.

"Because I'm a busy-ass career oriented woman working to make a name for myself in a field dominated by men, and your job is to look gorgeous and let people take pictures of you."

Juliet rolled her eyes as they sat down. "That's hard work too, and you know it."

Noemi squeezed her hand across the

table. "I know it is. I'm just giving you shit. How have you been?"

"Just got back from a photoshoot in Rome," Juliet said, picking up the menu. "I'm jetlagged as fuck. How are *you*?"

"Busy, but I like it that way," Noemi said. "Eli and I have a guest for a few weeks."

"Whaa-at?" Juliet said, arching her eyebrows comically high. "You and the golden boy let someone into the inner circle? Who is this miracle worker, and are they single?"

"His name is Rune," Noemi said, fighting a laugh. "He's a new d-man for the Kingfishers and needed a place to stay. I like him, honestly. Didn't expect to—we weren't really ready for guests and you know how we are, but...." She shrugged. "It's been nice. He's only been with us for two days, and they're gone on a road trip, but he's super chill."

"Have you talked to Eli yet?"

Noemi fidgeted with her fork. "No."

"That ever gonna happen?" Juliet's tone was deceptively casual.

Noemi sighed. "I don't know."

"Well, at least you're honest. With me, if not him."

"I just—how am I supposed to tell him I'm not really interested in sex? It feels nice but it's not something I *want*, and that's not fair to him. He's so good to me, Juju, and I'm not living up to my side of things."

"Bullshit." Juliet's voice was flat. "What's not *fair* to him is lying to him. Which is what you're doing."

Noemi flinched. "Aren't we supposed to spend time catching up before you start tearing into all my life decisions?"

"That's not the kind of friends we are," Juliet said. "But fine, we'll play it your way. Tell me all about Archer. Is he housebroken yet?"

Noemi scowled at her but took the offered out.

THAT NIGHT, she took her salmon and vegetables into the living room to watch the game, Archer on her heels. The announcers were in full swing as she settled onto the couch, tucking her feet beneath her.

The camera zoomed in on Eli, shaving down his crease, and Noemi watched his body language. His movements were a little stiff, muscles tense like something was bothering him. Was it physical? He hadn't mentioned he was injured. Noemi leaned forward, absently fending Archer off as she focused.

The announcers were talking about his save percentage but Noemi barely heard them. Eli dropped to the ice and stretched, flexible as ever, and Noemi relaxed slightly. Whatever it was, it wasn't physical.

Skaters swirled around the crease and the camera cut away to go to an on-ice interview with Seth. Noemi sat up.

"Something's up with your father," she told Archer, who pricked his ears, clearly hoping for fish.

Rune flashed past the camera, moving so fast he was recognizable only by the number 94 on his back, and the announcer asked Seth about him.

"He's great," Seth said, voice almost drowned out by the music and fans. "We're really lucky to have him. He's meshing well with us. Can't wait to see what he brings to the table."

The announcer let him go and Seth gave her a relieved smile and skated off.

Noemi settled back into the cushions to eat, watching for any glimpse of Eli.

Rune *was* meshing well, she saw immediately. He had excellent chemistry with his d-partner, Ilya, and they already seemed to know instinctively where the other was.

The Wildfire was rebuilding, not enough depth on their defense and not fast enough on their offense. Every once in awhile they showed a flash of brilliance—Noemi had her eye on Nathan Tanaka in particular, a young Japanese-American forward who'd just gotten signed and was already proving to be a formidable opponent—but overall they were out of sync, sloppy with their line changes, and their shots on goal were embarrassingly low.

Which made it all the more concerning when Eli let in three in the first period. The camera zoomed in on him after every one as the Wildfire celebrated and Eli sprayed his face with water from his bottle. He showed no emotion, but then, he rarely did on the ice. Still, Noemi could read the frustration simmering in him.

The buzzer sounded and the teams headed off the ice. Rune leaned in and said something to Eli as they went down the tunnel, and then the camera cut away again.

Noemi was left seething with worry. She muted the television as the announcers came on to diagram the plays of the first period and probably to tear her husband's performance apart, and picked up her phone.

She turned it over in her hands, wishing she could call him but knowing he wouldn't be able to answer. She nearly dropped it when it rang, Eli's name flashing across the screen, but answered on the first ring.

"Eli?"

"Hey." Eli sounded tired. "I don't have long."

"What's wrong?" Noemi asked.

Eli sighed. There wasn't much background noise—he must have slipped into a quiet room. "Nothing. I mean… I just… needed to hear your voice."

"I'm right here," Noemi said. "Rune's fitting well. How's it feel from where you are?"

"Good," Eli said. "I'm letting him down, though."

"Don't," Noemi said sharply. "Don't think like that. Whatever's bothering you, it can wait, okay? Put it away for now. Lock it in a box. Not forever—just until the game is over. Can you do that for me?"

Eli made a quiet noise of agreement.

"We'll figure it out together," Noemi told him. "You're my person, Eli McKenna. No matter what happens, that will always be true."

"You're my person too," Eli said, nearly inaudible. "I love you, Nomes."

"I love you too," Noemi said. "Go back in there and show 'em how it's done. And watch your angles, they're sloppy."

Eli was laughing as he hung up, and Noemi smiled to herself.

He was a brick wall the rest of the game, his angles sharp and lethal, every move precisely calculated. The Wildfire players were clearly getting more and more frustrated as Eli blocked every attempt they made to put one home, and the rest of the Kingfishers were just as obviously galvanized. Seth scored first, then Jay on a breakaway, and then Rune, parked in front of the Wildfire goalie, tipped one in off an assist from Seth.

The third period was a tense, tight battle, both teams determined to claw out one more goal and pull ahead. But it was the Kingfishers' second line who scored two minutes before the final buzzer, Arseni feeding a pass to Evan, who fired it to Rudd. It deflected off his stick and between the goalie's knees, and Noemi punched the air as the team celebrated.

When the buzzer sounded, everyone lined up to congratulate Eli. Noemi couldn't see much of his face, but he was smiling, she could tell. Rune cupped his helmet and pressed their foreheads together briefly, and Eli's smile was even wider when he pulled away.

"Aww," Noemi said aloud, rubbing Archer's ears. "Daddy's making friends, look at him!"

ELI CALLED her two hours later, as she was drifting off to sleep in their bed.

"Shit, did I wake you?" he asked when she answered.

"Nah," Noemi said, stretching. "Maybe a bit. You did good, babe."

"My angles better?" Eli teased.

Noemi huffed a laugh, eyes closed. "Much. How're you feeling?"

"Good. Better, anyway. Thanks for listening."

"Kick the Direwolves' asses and come home, yeah?"

"You got it. Go to sleep."

"Love you," Noemi said, and fell asleep before Eli answered.

5

Rune

The Direwolves weren't going to go down without a fight. Rune could tell that the minute they stepped on the ice. He'd played them enough to know they wouldn't hesitate to play dirty to get the win.

Sure enough, they were barely five minutes in before Seth got boarded roughly by a Wolves' d-man, hitting the wall at an angle and going down hard.

The linesmen got there first, before any of the Kingfishers could drop gloves and challenge him, and the offending d-man skated for the box, laughing. His jersey said TAYLOR. He had dirty blond hair and a mean twist to his mouth. Rune hated him on sight.

Three minutes after he got out of the box, Taylor snowed Eli. Arseni grabbed him and dragged him backward, but they were separated before anything happened, as Eli brushed melting ice off his jersey with no expression on his face.

On the bench, Rune clutched his stick, jaw tight.

Jay scored at the beginning of the second period—Rune could see flashes of brilliance in the young rookie, and he hoped he'd be around long enough to see him develop—and came by the bench for his fist-bumps with a huge grin on his face.

The battle continued, up and down the ice. Their top line tied the game, then pulled ahead by one as the Kingfishers struggled to hold on and regain the lead.

Halfway through the third period, Taylor barreled in with a puck on a breakaway, the Kingfishers giving fruitless chase as Eli came out to meet him. Taylor bore down fast and hard and Rune, trying desperately to catch him, had only a split-second to realize he wasn't going to stop before he plowed right into Eli and sent them both sprawling into the net.

Rune skidded to a stop and bodily hauled Taylor up and off. The actual fight was a blur. Taylor's fists were hard but his swings undisciplined, emotion clearly ruling his punches. Rune tucked his head, let the blows rain down on his shoulders, and then tightened his grip on Taylor's jersey and hammered him hard with his right fist.

It was over in a matter of seconds, Taylor losing his balance and pulling Rune down on top of him. Taylor was shouting something, lips peeled off bloody teeth in a snarl, but Rune couldn't hear him, the roar in his ears only rivaled by that of the crowd.

The linesmen dragged them apart and Rune glanced at Eli over his shoulder as he was escorted away. Eli was watching him, expression as unreadable as ever. He didn't look hurt.

"Seattle number ninety-four, five minute major for fighting," the ref announced. "Denver number twenty-two, two minute minor for fighting, two minute minor for goaltender interference."

Taylor blew Rune a kiss through the glass. Rune elected not to notice.

They lost the game by two, the final goal scored by Taylor while Rune served his last minute on the penalty and seethed silently.

In the locker room after cooldowns, Rune kept his media mask in place as the reporters grilled him about what he'd been thinking, why he'd been so aggressive in his defense of Eli.

"He's my goalie," he said, lifting one shoulder. "You have to protect your goalie. Goes double for d-men. That's my job, staying between him and the enemy." He caught sight of Eli over a reporter's shoulder, surrounded by his own scrum of media, and faltered. "You know, on the ice."

"So you don't regret it?"

"Well, I regret losing," Rune said ruefully, making them smile. "But I don't regret standing up for Reaper."

Coach spent most of the bus ride back to the airport yelling at Rune, which might have been why Eli didn't speak to him until they were on the plane, settled in their seats. He didn't *look* mad, Rune thought, sneaking a careful glance at him, but then, he'd already learned Eli was a master at hiding his emotions. People saw what he wanted them to see.

Buckled and waiting for the engines to spin up, Eli folded his hands in his lap and delicately cleared his throat.

"That wasn't necessary."

"Yes it was," Rune said.

Eli sighed through his nose. "Coach will have your ass if you make a habit of that."

"Tell the players on other teams not to run over you and I won't make a habit of it," Rune countered.

Eli's lips twitched. "Thank you, in any case. But really, *don't* do that again."

"Sure, bud," Rune said, getting comfortable and lacing his hands across his stomach. "As long as no one else runs over you."

Eli sighed again and Rune closed his eyes to the sight of him fighting the smile.

THEY RODE home from the airport in exhausted silence, Rune's head propped on his fist. Eli was frowning as he drove, concentrating on the road, which was thankfully empty of traffic. His profile was backlit in gold from the streetlights, and he muttered something under his breath as Rune watched him, half-asleep.

"Noemi's probably asleep," Eli said in the driveway.

Rune put a finger to his lips. "Not a peep."

But Noemi was in the living room, scrambling to her feet as Eli opened the door. She got to Eli first and pulled him into a fierce hug as Rune closed the door behind them.

"Hi, hi," she said, laughing softly. "Hi, I've missed you, how are you?"

Eli kissed her, quick and brief, and

straightened. "Good," he said, smiling down at her. "Glad to be home."

Noemi turned to Rune, arms out, and Rune blinked as she gathered him into a hug, going up on tiptoes to get her arms around his neck. She was soft and smelled sweet like honeysuckle, her hair tickling his cheek.

"Welcome home," she said when she let him go, and Rune couldn't help smiling back at her. "And thank you," Noemi continued, "for protecting my husband."

Eli rolled his eyes and headed down the hallway. "Don't need protecting," he called over his shoulder, and Noemi winked at Rune.

"Seriously," she said, lowering her voice. "He intimidates the rookies, and he's so closed off he has a hard time connecting even with the vets. You standing up for him is good. Hopefully the others will follow your lead more."

Rune nodded, shouldering his bag as Noemi gave him another smile and turned to follow Eli. How anyone could meet Eli and not realize he needed protection was beyond him, he mused as he made his way down the hall to his bedroom. It'd taken a handful of minutes in Eli's company to see the wall he put up to guard himself, and the shy, lonely man on the other side of it.

He crawled into bed, relaxing against honeysuckle-scented sheets with a relieved sigh, still thinking about the look on Eli's face.

Rune was no cheater. He got the impression Eli wasn't either, even if he *wasn't* straight, something Rune wouldn't bet on. As attractive as Eli was, as enticing the line of his jaw and the scope of his shoulders, he was off-limits. Rune would respect that. No flirting, no checking him out, nothing that hinted to his deep attraction.

Because they could be friends, and for that, Rune was grateful. The attraction he felt went far below surface appearance—he genuinely liked Eli and wanted to be around him as much as possible. But he could—and *would*—keep it platonic. Eli needed friends. Rune was happy to be able to give him that.

He rolled over and fell asleep thinking about Eli's smile.

6

Noemi

"Have you talked to him yet?"

Noemi sighed. "Hi Ju. Can we not do this right now?"

"Nope." Juliet sounded cheerful, a raucous blend of voices in the background. "I'm your best friend, bitch. You're clearly not getting past this without help. Enter *moi*."

"He's busy!" Noemi protested. "*I'm* busy, dammit. Did you know we have a chance at The Frozen Four this year? That hasn't happened in at least thirty years. Do you have any idea what it would mean for us to make it with a female coach?"

"Nomes."

Noemi stared up at the ceiling of her very cramped office and prayed for patience. "Soon," she finally said.

"It's been a month since our lunch date, and you've been saying that every time we've talked since."

"I know. I *know*. But like… how he feels affects how well he does his job. If I tell him and it upsets him, then it's my fault the Kingfishers start losing, and I don't need that kind of guilt."

"You really think he's unstable enough to let it fuck up his game?" Juliet asked.

"It might, you don't know," Noemi shot back. "Plus it's harder to find time with Rune there. Not that I mind having him—actually weirdly the opposite. The morning after they got home from their roadie, Eli and I got up and he'd taken Archer out for a run. It's their routine now. Archer loves him. He cuddles with Rune more than he does us, I swear. And he cooks, did I tell you? He made us bratwurst and spatzle the other day and he makes these German pancakes that are out of this *world* good, he's on permanent breakfast duty because of it."

"He still hasn't found a place?" Juliet sounded thoughtful.

"It's only been a couple of weeks," Noemi said. She knew she sounded defensive but she couldn't help it. "He was looking at a place but it got rented almost immediately. Plus he's just as busy and I told you—we like having him there."

"Huh."

"Don't you 'huh' me," Noemi said.

"I'm not doing anything!" Juliet protested.

"Yes you are, I know that tone of voice. You're psychoanalyzing me again. Just because you got a degree in psychology doesn't mean you get to just… do that. So knock it off."

"Well, it's just interesting, isn't it," Juliet began, and Noemi pinched the bridge of her nose. "Here you are sleeping separately until Rune shows up, but in a very happy, solid relationship, even though it's comparatively sexless. And now you're sharing a bed with Eli, and Rune's in your bedroom but you don't seem to mind. You are, in fact, comfortable with this arrangement, unless I miss my guess by a country mile."

"Don't try to be southern, it's not cute," Noemi snapped.

"But am I wrong?"

Noemi sighed loudly.

"Exactly." Juliet sounded smug.

"Don't get me wrong, I want my room back," Noemi said. "If we had a three bedroom house, and I could do it without making Rune ask questions, I'd be right back to having my own bed. But…. I don't know. He makes it easy. He's never in the way, he's really quiet, and did I mention Archer loves him?"

"Couple of times."

"Plus he and Eli are becoming friends. They like the same stuff, and Rune sticks up for him even off the ice; you know how the rookies are terrified of E? Well, Rune sort of… smooths his rough edges. Makes him a little less intimidating, I guess. They hang out together when I'm stuck at work or whatever."

"God, this just gets more and more interesting," Juliet mused. "Eli doesn't *do* friends."

"Yes he does," Noemi said. "You're just still mad because he doesn't want to be *your* friend."

"I'm delightful and he should *be* so lucky," Juliet retorted. "I just think it's interesting, is all."

"Whatever. I've got actual work to do, so can we wrap this up?"

"This isn't over," Juliet warned. "And talk to your goddamn husband, would you?"

"Come to dinner tomorrow night, *bye*," Noemi said loudly, and hung up.

She hadn't been lying—they'd all been so busy Noemi hadn't found a decent time to bring anything up. They were all exhausted pretty much all the time, and Noemi didn't want to spoil their precious days off by introducing difficult topics.

Besides, she liked Rune. More importantly, she liked the way Eli opened up around him. Something about Rune's personality made Eli blossom. He was more comfortable, chatty with him in a way he never was with anyone but Noemi, even relaxing enough to let his wicked sense of humor shine.

It delighted Noemi to see Eli smiling more, letting his guard down and allowing himself to enjoy someone else's company, and if that meant keeping Rune around awhile longer, she was okay with that, she decided.

She pushed open the front door and Archer came bounding down the hall to greet her. "I'm home!" Noemi called, bending to pet Archer, who wriggled happily under her hands.

There was a thud, a grunt, and the sound of something heavy falling. Noemi went in the direction of the noises and stopped dead in the doorway to the living room, eyebrows skyrocketing.

"What the fuck," she said blankly.

The furniture had been pushed to the edges of the room, her Persian rug carefully rolled up and set on end in one corner. In the middle of the resulting open space, Rune had Eli in a headlock, on his knees as Eli flailed in a desperate attempt to get free.

"What the *fuck*," Noemi repeated, louder, and Rune glanced over his shoulder.

"Hi!" he said cheerfully. "I'm teaching your husband to fight."

Eli waved one hand, most of his body hidden behind Rune's bulk.

"Why does my husband need to know how to fight?" Noemi inquired. She took her shoes off and leaned against the doorway. "E, you planning on throwing down with another goalie?"

"Mmph—no," Eli managed, voice muffled. He wriggled again but Rune didn't loosen his grip. "But Rune said I should at least know how to in case anyone tries to start something."

"Uh huh. And how's that working for you?"

"He's kicking my ass," Eli grumbled, sounding disgruntled, and Rune laughed and released him.

"Glad to see you're getting along so

well," Noemi said, bending to pick up her shoes. "Please put my living room back together when you're done. Eli, Juliet's coming over for dinner tomorrow night."

Eli scrambled to his feet and brushed himself off. He looked dismayed. "Why?"

Noemi raised one eyebrow. "Because she's my best friend and I haven't seen her in over a month and also she wants to meet Rune."

Eli muttered something under his breath and Rune looked quizzical.

"Should I dress up?" he inquired.

"God, no," Noemi said. "Wear whatever you want, it's just Juliet." She left, smiling to herself as she padded down the hall to the bedroom and was pulling on a pair of leggings when Eli let himself into the room.

"Hi!" she said.

Eli closed the distance between them and wrapped his arms around her waist.

"Hey," Noemi said softly, touching his hair as he pressed his face against her throat. "Hey, what's bothering you?"

Eli didn't say anything at first, holding her tight. "Maybe I just missed you," he finally said, lifting his head.

Noemi smiled up at him. "How was practice?"

"Good." Eli released her and sat down on the edge of the bed as Noemi went back to tugging the leggings up over her hips. "Your dad is swapping lines around again, keeping things interesting. What about you?"

Noemi groaned and pulled her favorite sleeveless shirt from the drawer. "If we could just drive home the *importance* of how close we are to being in the running, that'd be fucking great. But all they want to do is drink and sleep around. There are like… three players who're treating this seriously. One of them I've got my eye on for the Kingfishers—he's gonna be seriously good when he grows into himself."

"You should come coach us instead," Eli said, eyes gleaming with amusement.

"God, I would *love* that, but can you imagine the nepotism talk?" Noemi mock-shuddered. "Father, daughter, *and* son-in-law all on the same team? The minute we lost a single game, people would be screaming for our heads."

Eli grimaced. "Fair enough. But it'd be nice to have you there."

"I'll come to practice soon," Noemi promised, sitting down beside him. "I want to see how you guys are meshing as a team anyway. How's Rune working out?"

"He's probably the best d-man we've got," Eli said honestly. "He gives the others confidence, they try harder because they see how much he puts into every single practice, let alone our games."

Noemi put her head on his shoulder. "And are you okay with him still being here?"

Eli didn't move for a minute. "I mean," he said cautiously. "He… fits, doesn't he?"

"Yeah," Noemi agreed. She looked up into his face. "I love that he runs with Archer when we've got other stuff going on. And god, I want him to make those pancakes again, what are they called?"

"*Kaiserschmarrn*," Eli said, a smile playing on his lips. "Even though he's in your room?"

Noemi shrugged. "I told Juliet earlier today that if we had a three bedroom house and I could do it without him questioning our relationship, I'd suggest he stay forever. I like having him here, babe. He's funny and thoughtful and sweet, and it doesn't hurt that he's easy on the eyes."

"Behave," Eli said, lips twitching. "Should I be worried?"

"What, that I'll dump your ass and run off with him?" Noemi pretended to consider. "I mean, he *does* do the dishes without being asked—"

"So do I!" Eli protested, clearly wounded, and Noemi burst out laughing.

"Aw baby, don't look at me like that. I've

got you housebroken and everything—no way am I trading you in now."

Eli grumbled, but his lips were twitching. "So, Juliet, huh?"

"She's *so* excited to see you," Noemi said, hopping up off the bed and bending to drop a quick kiss on Eli's forehead.

"So she can drag me for all my life choices again?" Eli muttered. He followed her out of the bedroom and down the hall to the kitchen.

"You know she only does that because she cares," Noemi tossed over her shoulder. She raised her voice. "Rune!"

Rune stuck his head out of the living room, looking quizzical.

"Steaks tonight, you up to manning the grill?"

"Oh hell yeah," Rune said, grinning. "Let me just finish up in here and I'll go fire it up."

"I should help him," Eli said. He sounded faintly guilty. He dropped a quick kiss on her shoulder and brushed past her down the hall to disappear into the living room.

Eli

"So who's Juliet?" Rune inquired as Eli helped him push the sofa back into position.

"College friend," Eli huffed. Damn Rune, he wasn't even out of breath. "Psychology major, so she *will* analyze you and put all your complexes and insecurities on display for the world to see."

"Oh, so *that's* why you don't like her."

"It's not a matter of 'liking' her," Eli protested, grabbing the overstuffed chair and dragging it back into place. "Noemi loves her, so of course she's a good person. She just... sees more than I'd like, maybe."

"What does she see?" Rune asked softly. He was standing in the middle of the living room, wearing comfortable pants, a faded Kingfishers shirt, and brightly colored socks. He looked rumpled, soft, but Eli remembered all too well the steel of his muscles as he pinned Eli in place, keeping him there with seemingly no effort at all.

Eli gathered his thoughts and shrugged, bending to pick up a throw pillow and tossing it back on the sofa. "Just... stuff."

"Well, how about I keep her focused on me?" Rune suggested. He handed Eli another pillow and Eli put it in position.

"Oh, she'll definitely cross-examine you," Eli said. "But I imagine she'll save some energy to dissect me some more too."

"Like how?" Rune asked.

"Like why am I okay with the salary I accepted from the Kingfishers, and do I ever think about getting therapy for the way I grew up, and my obvious daddy issues, and when's the last time I was actually honest with Noemi about what I want. Things like that."

Rune's eyebrows were in his hairline. "Jesus Christ."

"Sorry," Eli said guiltily. "She's actually really nice, I swear. She's funny as hell and she has great taste and she's so, so loyal to Noemi. I think you'll like her, really."

Rune looked dubious. "If you say so."

"I'll make sure she goes easy on you," Eli told him.

"My hero." Rune grinned, bumping him with his shoulder and following him to the kitchen.

7

Rune

"Nomes, I hope you don't mind," Juliet said, her voice carrying into the living room where Eli and Rune were sitting. "But poor Maxime was all on his own, didn't have anywhere to go and I couldn't just *leave* him alone in a foreign city. He barely speaks English, poor lamb!"

She appeared in the doorway, Noemi peeking past her. She was tall, at least an inch taller than Eli, with cheekbones that could cut steel highlighted by jet black hair in a choppy pixie cut and obsidian skin that glowed with health. She examined Rune with sharp eyes the color of onyx, and Rune had the impression she wasn't missing a thing.

"Rune, Juliet," Noemi said. "And apparently, Maxime. Hi, Maxime, welcome to our home."

Juliet stepped out of the way and Maxime was revealed behind her. He was tall, pale, and thin, with cheekbones to rival Juliet's and hair pulled up in a messy bun. The light from the lamps and fireplace danced on the sharp angles of his face.

"He's French," Juliet said helpfully.

Rune stood and held out a hand. "Welcome to Seattle," he said in French, and Maxime's smoky gray eyes went wide.

"You speak my beautiful language!"

Rune laughed. "I don't practice as much as I should, but I grew up with a French family next door and picked it up before I was out of diapers."

Maxime was glowing with delight. "To hear it spoken again—Juliet tries but she's terrible. You, though—you sound like home. And I thought you'd just be another, what is the word—" He gestured. "Dumb jock!" he said in English and Rune stiffened.

He was aware of the others listening but he didn't look at them. "Appearances can be deceiving," he said, keeping his tone light. "How do you like Seattle?"

This was apparently the opening Maxime had been waiting for. Noemi got everyone sitting down and comfortable as Maxime told Rune at length how rude

Americans were, how smelly the city was, how awful the traffic, until Rune was gritting his teeth to hold back the sharp comment.

Juliet was talking to Eli, and Rune swallowed guilt. He'd promised to keep Juliet's attention on him instead, and he wasn't delivering.

He waited until Maxime stopped complaining to take a drink of the wine Noemi had brought in to turn to Juliet.

"So," he said, and Juliet fixed her sharp eyes on him, one lethal eyebrow going up. "How long have you and Noemi been friends?"

"Grade school," Juliet said, mouth quirking. "I stole her crayon, she pulled my hair. Best friends ever since."

"Never did get that damn crayon back," Noemi muttered.

Juliet's smile was brilliant. "Got the best friend you'll ever have, though." She glanced at Eli. "Except for you, of course."

"Uh huh." Eli's tone was dry but he didn't seem too upset as Juliet switched her focus back to Rune.

"Tell us about yourself," she said. "Are you single? Anyone back in—fuck, where'd you get traded from?"

"Atlanta," Rune said, amused. "I'm single. Not really looking for anything." He hesitated. He hated lying, even through omission, but even more, he hated the internal battle he fought every time he decided to come out to someone. Was Juliet safe? Would she out him? What about Maxime? He shook his head at his own internal debate. He trusted Noemi, and Noemi trusted Juliet. That was all there was to it. "I'm not publicly out, so it makes dating a little harder."

Juliet sipped her wine, gaze assessing. Beside her, Maxime looked more alert, eyes raking over Rune's body with an almost physical touch.

Noemi coughed. "I have to go make the salad. Juju, you're with me."

"But I want to talk to Rune," Juliet protested.

"Tough."

Juliet growled and stood with fluid grace, following Noemi from the room and muttering under her breath.

Alone with Maxime, Rune and Eli traded looks. Eli shrugged fractionally and took a drink. *Traitor*, Rune thought vengefully as Maxime scooted nearer.

"So," he said, tracing the rim of his glass with one long finger. "I hear that hockey players have a lot of… stamina."

He was way too sober, Rune decided, and set about remedying that.

Eli

Laughter pealed from the kitchen, Juliet and Noemi clearly having a wonderful time. In the living room, Maxime was plastered up against Rune's side, toying with the hem of his shirt and looking at him through his lashes.

Eli stood abruptly, making Rune twitch. Maxime didn't even seem to notice. "Gonna go help Nomes." He was gone before Rune could say anything.

Noemi was shredding spinach, Juliet nowhere in sight. She smiled as Eli came in. "Juliet's in the bathroom. Where are the others?"

"They're making their own fun," Eli said shortly, and pulled a beer from the refrigerator. When he turned back, though, Noemi didn't look any happier than he felt, her dark brows furrowed and eyes troubled.

"Rune and… Maxime?" she said.

Eli shrugged. "I guess."

Noemi put her hands on the counter. "But—"

"But what?" Eli said. "He's an adult. Just because I don't like Maxime doesn't mean Rune can't have fun with him."

"You don't like him either?" Noemi asked, briefly diverted.

"He sneers at us," Eli said, resting a hip against the counter. "I may not be able to speak French but I can understand more than he realizes. And he called us dumb jocks, you heard that."

"Ugh, yeah." Noemi washed her hands, frowning. "This is weird. I don't like it. I'm going to put a stop to it."

She marched for the door and Eli caught her around the waist, pulling her to a stop.

"Adult, Nomes," he reminded her. "He wasn't exactly shoving the guy away. You can't just go in there and cockblock them because you don't like someone."

"Says you," Noemi muttered mutinously. She grabbed Eli's hands. "Rune shouldn't *be* with him, E. You know that."

"I know we can't decide that for him," Eli said. "Even though I agree."

"Agree with what?" Juliet asked, fingers busy on her phone as she sauntered into the kitchen.

"With the wine I chose for dinner," Noemi said immediately.

Eli widened his eyes at her. *Lying to your best friend?*

Noemi stuck her tongue out at him and Eli laughed, patting her arm. "What do you need me to help with?"

Dinner was about as awkward as Eli had expected, with Maxime draped over Rune, who seemed amused by his blatant flirting. Every time Maxime touched Rune's arm, marveling over his muscles or how soft his skin was, Eli clenched his teeth a little harder, but Rune didn't push him away, didn't ask him to stop. He just ate his quinoa and salmon and discussed diet plans with Juliet and smiled at Eli when their eyes met.

Juliet seemed almost charmed by him, something Eli hadn't thought possible. She propped her elbows on the table and had a serious discussion about a new diet fad sweeping through Europe, and its potential for burning fat and building lean muscle. Maxime had both hands wrapped around Rune's bicep, his head on Rune's shoulder as they talked, but Rune didn't even seem to notice.

Eli met Noemi's eyes. She looked as miserable as he felt.

Maxime and Juliet lingered after dessert, until Eli's skin was crawling with the need for them to be *gone*, out of his space, Maxime with his predatory eyes and Juliet's silent judgment.

When they finally left, Maxime pulled Rune to the side, went up on tiptoe, and whispered something in his ear. Whatever he said, Rune's eyes went wide and a flush crawled up his throat as Maxime stepped back, smiling brilliantly up at him.

Eli set his jaw and said nothing. Juliet laughed and hugged Noemi, gave Eli a wave, and kissed Rune on the cheek.

The house was silent for a moment after the door closed, all three looking at each other.

"I'm going to clean up," Rune said, and headed for the kitchen.

Clean up was done in silence, Eli biting back the questions. *Did you get his number? Are you going to sleep with him?*

When they were done, Rune dried his hands and straightened. "Goodnight."

Eli and Noemi looked at each other after he left the room and finally Noemi sighed.

"Being a grownup sucks."

Noemi

The next day was a day off for Eli and Rune, but not for Noemi. When she came out to the kitchen, there was coffee on the counter and an omelette in the warmer for her. Eli and Rune were sitting at the table, Eli with his head on his arm and Rune with his elbows on the table and chin in hand. They both looked mostly asleep, and Noemi smiled to herself as she poured coffee and gathered her belongings.

"Enjoy your day off," she said brightly, and Eli mumbled something.

Noemi laughed and dropped a kiss on his cheek, then turned to Rune and did the same thing as he tilted his face up absently.

She didn't realize what she'd done until she was halfway to work.

"Oh my god." She fumbled for the phone. "Call Juliet," she ordered it.

"Nomes?" Juliet sounded asleep herself.

"I kissed Rune!" Noemi blurted.

"You fucking *what*?" Juliet sounded much more awake suddenly.

Noemi gripped the steering wheel so tightly the leather creaked. "I kissed. Rune," she said through her teeth.

"You—but—I thought he was gay?"

"He *is*. It wasn't like that, I was getting breakfast and he and Eli were in the kitchen and I kissed Eli's cheek and then Rune was right there so I kissed him too, I didn't even *think* about it, it just *happened*, oh my god—"

"Breathe," Juliet ordered. "So, not on

the mouth. Not romantic in any way, right?"

"No." Noemi took the next exit and found a gas station with available parking. "No, it wasn't—I was just saying goodbye like I do to Eli every day. Only I did it to Rune by accident too. That was so *inappropriate* of me, Ju, he's probably horribly embarrassed—"

"Oh stop," Juliet snapped. "I saw him last night. He likes you a lot. He likes Eli more, but the important thing is, he's comfortable with you. He wouldn't still be living in your house if he wasn't. So what if you pecked him on the cheek? It's not like you slipped him some tongue."

Noemi shuddered. "I have to apologize."

"Or you could *not* do that," Juliet said. "Since you haven't done anything worth apologizing for."

"Still—"

"I'm not saying don't talk about it," Juliet interrupted. "Just… don't go into it acting like you've done a horrible thing, because you *haven't*. How long has he been there now?"

"Like… six weeks. No, seven."

"Still no plans to move out?"

"Why is this your business?" Noemi snapped.

"I'm just curious," Juliet protested. "Answer the question, come on."

Noemi sighed. "He's made a few comments about looking for somewhere, but he's tired a lot, okay? They're playing really hard. It's not surprising he hasn't had the energy to do a serious house-hunt."

"Uh huh. Or maybe he likes living with you guys more than you realize."

"Don't be ridiculous. I have to go."

"Talk to him but don't apologize," Juliet said, and hung up.

8

Noemi got home somehow. Honestly, the whole day was kind of a blur in her memory, most of her brainpower dedicated to playing out different conversations in her head. The commute home was almost entirely on autopilot, and before she knew it she was standing in front of the door.

She didn't allow herself to pause, because the only thing more potentially excruciating than this conversation would have been standing outside her own door all evening, frozen in her tracks by social anxiety and a naggingly familiar fear.

"I'm home!" Her voice sounded normal, she thought, despite the emotions trying to choke it out. As usual, Archer was the first to greet her, wriggling with joy. *So that's one,* Noemi thought wryly, crouching down to give him the attention he deserved. Hopefully the rest of her housemates were equally glad to see her.

"In the kitchen!" Eli's voice floated down the hall toward her.

Noemi couldn't sense anything different in his voice. Straightening to her not-very-considerable height, she reminded herself that she was the kind of person who faced things head-on.

Ignoring the voice which sounded suspiciously like Juliet inside her head, she took the first step toward the kitchen.

She paused in the doorway for a second. *Not postponing things*, she told herself. *Just watching*. Rune was sliding a pan of vegetables into the oven as Eli turned from the refrigerator, a package of salmon filets in his hands. Rune was clearly mid-anecdote, his free hand moving as he talked. Eli was smiling, not the small, guarded thing she usually saw around other people, but the real one, the one he usually reserved for her.

Despite the upcoming conversation—which they were definitely going to have—something in Noemi's chest relaxed from where it had been clenched tight all day.

Before she could parse the feeling, Archer wriggled around her legs and burst into the kitchen, drawing their eyes.

"Hey, Nomes." Eli set the salmon on the counter and crossed to give her a hug. "We thought we'd handle dinner tonight. How was work?"

"Oh, you know." Noemi stretched up to kiss his cheek, hugging him back maybe a little harder than she'd planned. "It was work. I didn't murder any idiot college boys and nobody puked on the ice. But I'm ready to be home."

Eli squeezed back before letting go, his arms a familiar comfort around her. "Well, have a seat and your househusbands will have dinner on the table shortly."

The plural was so subtle that for a moment she wasn't sure she'd actually heard it. But when she snuck a look at Eli, he was wearing the shit-eating grin that said he'd decided to chirp her about this forever.

"What, no slippers and drink?" She settled herself in a chair at the table, trying to act like this was normal banter despite the heat in her cheeks. "Maybe I need new househusbands."

"But can they keep you in nutritionist-approved meals?" Rune's eyes were twinkling as he hung the oven mitt up on its hook.

Noemi's smile felt almost normal at the complete ease he was radiating. Despite Juliet's confidence, she'd more than half expected to walk into the kind of awkward silence that said they'd been talking about her. Or, worst-case, Eli alone, Rune already gone to find a new place to live.

"I guess I'd better keep the two of you around, then."

Her response was maybe a beat too late. Eli caught her eye, an eyebrow raised in silent question. She smiled reassurance at him, doing her best to convey that they could talk about it later.

When she looked away from Eli, Rune was giving her a nearly identical questioning but fond expression. It probably meant something that Noemi couldn't feel her smile changing when she looked at him, but it had been a long day with too much introspection already.

Nodding decisively, she startled a little when a glass of wine appeared on the table, Eli's hand landing on her shoulder and squeezing. "Here's a drink, just in case. Do you even have slippers?"

"Not after Archer shredded the last pair." Noemi took a sip, relaxing just slightly. "But since we're not going anywhere tonight, I'm gonna change while you two finish up in here."

Pushing to her feet, she wrapped her arms around Eli's waist, kissing his cheek. "Be right back."

She'd only taken a step toward the door before Eli cocked an eyebrow, fighting to keep the smile off his face. "No kiss for Rune? He's gonna think you don't love him as much."

Noemi narrowed her eyes at him and Eli's smile widened.

Asshole. That was how it was going to be? Two could play that game.

"Don't be silly, E." Noemi headed straight for where Rune stood in front of the stove. "I have plenty of love to go around."

She was prepared to back off at any sign of discomfort. But Rune just held out an arm in invitation when she was close enough, pulling her in and helping her balance as she went up on tiptoe to kiss his cheek, too.

"There." Noemi patted his arm and turned away, praying her face wasn't as red as it felt and sticking her tongue out at Eli with her back safely to Rune. "Be right back."

Maybe it was the wine, maybe it was the chirping and easy acceptance and Eli's laughter as she left the room, but she felt so light she could just about float to the bedroom.

Eli

Noemi was already in bed when Eli

emerged from the bathroom, snuggled in to her side, even though it still felt a little weird for her to have a side. "Want me to turn off the light?"

"You don't have to."

He wasn't quite sure what to make of that, so he compromised by turning off the overhead light and leaving the bedside lamp on as he crawled into bed to sit up against the headboard. "You should probably go to sleep. We shouldn't have started that movie so late."

Noemi made a small disgruntled noise. "Not sleepy. I wanna talk to you. We haven't talked—really *talked*—in forever."

"I'm sorry," Eli said, remorse prickling his skin. "What do you want to talk about? You kissing Rune?"

Noemi pinched his leg. "Leave me the fuck alone."

Eli laughed and rubbed his thigh. "I had to, you know that."

Noemi pressed her face against his hip. "I don't really care what we talk about," she confessed, voice muffled against Eli's pajamas. "I just… miss you."

God. Eli slid down in the bed until he was on his side facing her. Noemi smiled at him, her dark blue eyes luminous in the dimly lit room.

"I love you," Eli told her. "I wish I could

take some time off so we could be alone together for a bit."

Noemi's lips curved and she squeezed his hip. "I love you too. And it's okay. When the season's over, maybe we can go away for the summer."

Eli pecked her lightly on the nose. Did she want sex? It was so hard to tell with Noemi. Maybe he should just ask her, but if she said yes—guilt soured his stomach. This wasn't how it was supposed to be, loving his best friend, *marrying* his best friend, but barely able to touch her. *She has needs too*, he thought miserably. And he wasn't meeting them.

"Hey, hey," Noemi said, searching his face. "What's going on in that head of yours?"

Eli took a deep breath and shook his head. "Nothing. I'm just tired."

Noemi's eyes narrowed. "Do you remember our wedding vows?"

"Uh."

Of course he remembered.

I, Eli McKenna, promise to take you, Noemi Caron, as my lawful wedded wife. I promise to be your biggest cheerleader, your loudest supporter, the shoulder for you to cry on when the world is too much. I promise never to lie to you, to always tell you what's bothering me, to share my burdens when they're too much for me to carry.

Eli sighed, bracing himself like there was a center on a breakaway bearing down on him. "Do you wish we had sex more often?"

There. He'd said it. And from the way Noemi's eyes widened, she hadn't been expecting it.

She sat up, crossing her legs, and Eli followed suit, the separation leaving him suddenly chilled.

"Do *you* wish we had sex more often?" she asked.

Eli fidgeted.

"No lying," Noemi reminded him.

"How am I supposed to tell the truth without hurting your feelings?" Eli countered.

"So that's a yes." Noemi's face was unreadable.

"It's not *you*," Eli said, and then groaned. "Wow. Sorry, that was terrible. I didn't mean—"

"To be a cliche?" Noemi asked. She grinned suddenly and some of Eli's tension eased. "Come on, E, tell me what's going on. Is it bothering you that we only have sex a few times a month?"

Eli reached for her hand and Noemi curled her fingers around his, thumb stroking his knuckles. "We're both young," he said, feeling his way. "And, and… in love, right? I just worry that we're not—"

"Not what, living up to society's standards?" Noemi said. "We're both busy professionals. It's not really surprising we can't find a lot of time to be intimate. Besides, you know me. I just don't want it very much. And it's not *you*, either."

Eli half-laughed, squeezing her hand as she continued.

"I've *never* really wanted it, if we're being honest." Her expression turned thoughtful and she plucked at her nightgown with her free hand. "I thought… I *hoped* it would be different once we were married. I think you're hot, baby, I really do. But I just…." She sighed.

"Are you attracted to girls?" Eli asked gently.

Noemi gave this some thought, but finally shook her head. "I mean, I think they're hot too? God, I saw a girl yesterday who nearly made me choke on my own tongue. But it's like… ugh." She leaned forward, pressing her forehead to Eli's shoulder. "I didn't want to have sex with her," she mumbled.

Eli kissed her hair. It smelled like sweet honeysuckle. Some of the load was lifting from his heart. "I love you very much," he murmured.

"Love you too," Noemi sighed, and sat up. "Is it the same for you? You just don't want it?"

Eli hesitated. Could he tell her the truth? "I—" He stared at her hand, still in his. What if she hated him? What if she accused him of marrying her under false pretenses?

"You are the best friend I've ever had," Noemi said abruptly, and startled Eli into looking up. "I mean it," she continued. "Better than Juliet. Not even Monica in sixth grade holds a candle to you. I've never had anyone I trust like I do you—except maybe Adam, and he's off being disgustingly in love with Etienne."

Eli focused on her hand, her smooth skin, the tiny soft hair on her arms, hoping she hadn't seen his tiny flinch, the jealousy he'd felt watching Adam and Etienne together. He wasn't sure he could say the actual words.

"Are you gay?" Noemi asked, her voice gentle, and it was Eli's turn to fold forward, his face against her soft shoulder. Noemi cupped the back of his head, threading her fingers through his hair. "You know I don't love you any less, right?" she asked.

"Why *not*?" Eli demanded, sitting up. "I m-married you *knowing* I couldn't—" There was a lump in his throat so big he couldn't swallow around it. "I wanted to be normal," he whispered.

"Shame on you," Noemi said sharply.

Eli looked up, taken aback.

Her dark blue eyes snapped, holding him hostage. "How dare you say that about my husband? You think straight is the only way to be normal? Is there something wrong with Adam? With Tenny? What about Rune? Something wrong with me, because I think guys and girls are both hot?"

"No," Eli said, shaking his head desperately. "*No*, I didn't mean it that way, I didn't —fuck. Fuck, I'm sorry, Nomes, I just meant—"

"I know what you meant," Noemi said, and her voice was softer. "And I know you didn't mean it like that, but E, you can't think that way. Being gay—being anything other than straight, honestly—is just another way to be human. There's no such thing as normal. I love you exactly as you are."

"Even though I'm not sexually attracted to you?" The words felt like stones in Eli's throat, choking him with the weight of their truth.

"Oh baby," Noemi said, cupping his face. "The only thing that could make me love you less is if you… I don't know, killed someone or something."

Her hands were cool against Eli's burning cheeks. "Do you…." He swallowed hard, forcing the words out around the last of the lump in his throat. "Do you want a divorce?"

Noemi raised her eyebrows. "Do *you* want a divorce?"

Eli thought about it. Did he want to divorce his best friend and lose the life they were building together?

"No," he said abruptly. "I don't, I—fuck, Nomes, I love you. I love living with you, being *with* you. I don't want to lose that. Or you."

"Well good," Noemi said. She pulled his head down and pecked him on the nose before releasing him. "Because I don't either. Besides, from a purely pragmatic point of view, I think it helps us both to stay married, at least for awhile. You because you're not ready to come out, and me because dumbass preppy white boys are at least a *little* more inclined to listen to a married woman than they are a single one."

She tilted her head and smiled at him and Eli caught his breath.

"What about your needs?" he asked. "You deserve to have them met. If I can't give you what you need—"

"That's what a vibrator is for," Noemi interrupted, a wicked glint in her eyes. "I was taking care of my needs long before I met you, Eli. The real question is, what about *your* needs?"

For a moment, Eli had no idea what she meant. Then his brain caught up and his face caught fire. "I, uh—"

"I know it would be hard with not being out, but you know I know people." As usual, once Noemi got started, she was off full throttle. "If you wanted to go out, see if you meet someone you click with, I could come along and be your beard. Hell, I could set you up with someone—there's a really cute TA I see on campus sometimes, maybe he's single. And… open-minded."

The idea of going to a gay bar or even a deniably queer gathering was enough to objectively almost send Eli into a panic, but it was overwhelmed by the rush of love. "That's seriously above and beyond, Nomes."

"You've made me so happy." Noemi took his face in her hands. "You deserve to be happy too, baby."

Eli took a breath and held it, then let it out. "I don't deserve you."

She smiled, bright as the sunny yellow walls of her room. "No, I think we deserve each other just enough. If you don't want to start hunting for the man of your dreams, that's okay. I'll help whenever you're ready."

Eli studied her face. "You're seriously okay with me having sex with someone else."

"I mean, maybe not on our kitchen table," Noemi said thoughtfully, and startled Eli into a laugh. "Yeah, E, I seriously am," she continued, smiling back at him. "It's not going to change how much you love me, right?"

"Never," Eli said fiercely, pulling her close. "I will *never* stop loving you."

"Good. In that case, let's go to sleep. I don't know about you, but my brain stopped a while ago. I've been on autopilot all day."

"Like this morning when you kissed Rune?"

"Ugh." Noemi shoved him lightly. "Are you ever gonna let that go?"

Eli allowed himself to sway, grinning at her. "You like having him here. You're *comfortable* with him. I know how huge that is. I'm just teasing because it makes me happy."

Noemi wrinkled her nose. "This is cruel and unusual and probably breaking the Geneva Convention. I'm telling Dad."

"You wouldn't!"

Noemi's giggle pealed out, bright and joyful as ever.

Rune

Eli was in a good mood. He was more awake than usual, already cooking breakfast when Rune stumbled out, and greeted him with a bright smile. Rune blinked blearily at him and Eli's smile widened.

"Why are you so happy?" Rune asked warily.

Eli shrugged and flipped the omelet in the skillet. "Dunno. Just feel good. Plus it's game day. Playing the Birds. That always gets the crowd going. Local rivals and all that."

"Fuck." Rune collapsed at the table. "Quinn's gonna kick my ass again, you watch."

"Not if you don't touch Saint," Eli said comfortingly.

"That high stick was *not* my fault," Rune complained. "You think I'd be stupid enough to deliberately target Saint Hockey? I may be stupid but even I have limits."

"You're not stupid," Eli said, sounding like he was fighting a laugh as he slid a plate across the table to him. "Just consider yourself lucky you didn't make Saint bleed, or he probably would have killed you."

"Super reassuring," Rune muttered, and took a bite.

Eli settled opposite. His bearing was loose, amusement in his clear gray eyes, and Rune studied him over his eggs.

"What?" Eli said.

"Nothing. You're just not usually this… chipper."

Eli lifted a shoulder but he didn't tense up. "Noemi and I talked some stuff out last night. Good to clear the air, you know?"

"For sure," Rune said automatically. "Important in a relationship, all that good stuff." *What did you talk about?* He couldn't ask. Instead he applied himself to his breakfast, sneaking surreptitious looks at Eli as he ate.

Fuck's sake, Rune liked him more all the time. He liked the way he made snide comments during movies, the way he scrupulously cut the crusts off his toast, the way he cooed to Archer when he thought no one was listening.

The eggs turned to cold stone in his stomach and he set his fork down.

"You okay?" Eli asked.

Rune swallowed. "Yeah. Gonna… go get ready. Thanks for breakfast." He bolted before Eli could say anything else.

Safely in his bedroom, Rune sank onto the bed and clutched his head. Fuck, *fuck*. Somewhere along the way, he'd somehow developed a full-blown crush on Eli, and it was only getting worse. He'd thought—hoped, even knowing it was in vain—that proximity would lessen that gut-deep punch of attraction he'd felt the first time he'd seen Eli, but he should have known. He should have known living with him would only make him want him *more*.

"Stupid," he whispered, and tugged on his hair. He had to go, before it got worse. Feeling like this was a betrayal of not only Eli but also Noemi, both of whom had welcomed him into their home with nothing but good intentions.

After the game. He'd tell them how much he appreciated their generosity and then he'd get serious about looking for a place. His stomach twisted at the thought of leaving them but it had to be done.

9

Just like Eli had predicted, the arena was packed to capacity, the hometown crowd all turned out to support their team. On the way to the facility, Eli explained that the Seabirds vs. Kingfishers rivalry was a friendly one, but with the points from four games on the line, matches had a tendency to get chippy, players throwing their weight around a little more.

Rune participated in the usual game of two-touch beforehand with Eli, who was still smiling more than usual, less tightly wound. He even went so far as to tease Jay, who looked slightly stunned before retaliating in kind, the smile lighting up his face.

Still, he put his gear on with more of a return to his usual intensity. Something settled into place in Rune's chest, watching him frown into the middle distance as he strapped his chest pads on and jumped up and down a few times. The familiarity of his routine was like a balm to Rune's nerves. They might win, they might lose, Rune may or may not have fallen in love with him, but Eli would always suit up the same way. Twist to the right, shake his arm, twist to the left, shake his other arm, bend at the waist, bounce on his skates.

A ball of wadded up skate tape sailed by Rune's nose and he flinched, breaking out of his contemplative state. Jay gave him a cheeky grin and Rune flipped him off. Then it was time to file out, line up in the tunnel, wait for the music to spin up and warmups to start.

They were the usual blur. Rune focused on finding pucks and sending them at the net. Vanya took the crease first as Eli warmed up near the blue line, and Rune drifted over and dropped to his knees near him, white and teal jerseys whipping past on the other side.

Quinn skidded to a stop near them, still safely over the line. He was a big man with amber eyes that could harden to granite, which was also what his fists felt like. He cocked a sardonic eyebrow at Rune that told him clearly he hadn't forgotten their last encounter.

Eli's cough sounded suspiciously like a laugh and Rune glared at him.

"No high sticks this time, eh boys?" Quinn said conversationally.

"Do my very best," Rune promised, making Quinn's mouth twitch with amusement.

Saint flashed by, a streak of teal and white, and something in Quinn's eyes softened as he watched him go. Rune glanced at Eli—he hadn't missed it either, judging by his thoughtful expression.

Quinn tapped Eli's pad with his stick. "Let's have ourselves a hockey game, then!"

IT WAS A RESOUNDING DEFEAT. Saint scored in the first minute and a second line winger got lucky off a bad bounce just before the buzzer for the first period. On the other side of the ice, the Birds' goalie was a brick wall, stopping every shot with lethal accuracy and some of the most creative French cursing Rune had ever heard.

Eli's face gave nothing away, but his shoulders got tighter and tighter as time wound down and still no goals from the Kingfishers. Rune watched him when he wasn't on the ice, hunched forward with his elbows on his knees, dripping sweat and barely hearing Coach yelling.

Two minutes from the end of the final period and Saint's winger, Volkov, somehow slotted a puck right between Rune's skates. Eli flung himself sideways but it was too late—the puck hit the back of the net and the crowd groaned. It was over and everyone knew it, many of the fans getting up to leave before the final buzzer even sounded.

THE DRIVE HOME WAS DISMAL. Noemi had driven separately and was already home before they were even able to leave the arena. Rune watched Eli's profile, backlit by the golden glow of the streetlights. His mouth was downturned, no trace of the smile from earlier.

"I'm sorry," Rune said suddenly.

Eli flicked a glance at him. "It happens."

"I let you down," Rune insisted. "That Russian fucker got that shot on goal because I didn't block him. You depended on me to stop him and I didn't."

"Rune," Eli said flatly. "Shut up." His voice didn't hold a possibility of argument, and Rune shut up, miserable with defeat.

He dragged himself out of the car and followed Eli up the walk and into the house.

Archer greeted them and Eli bent to pet his ears, murmuring under his breath to him.

"In here," Noemi called from the living room. Eli glanced at Rune and they headed that direction in silence.

Noemi had turned the couch into… it looked like a nest, honestly. She'd pulled the extensions out, spread blankets over the segments, and supplemented with pillows she must have brought in from the bedroom. She was sitting in the middle of the arrangement, legs crossed and hands in her lap.

Rune stopped in the doorway, startled, but Eli didn't pause. He took his shoes off, dropped his suit jacket on the floor, and crawled onto the bedding. Noemi cupped his face briefly, eyes soft, and held out a hand to Rune.

Rune hesitated, but Noemi made an impatient gesture, still watching Eli, who was curling up in the mound of cushions. She pointed to Eli's other side and then lay down, tucking herself close as Rune took one shoe off and then the other, almost dazed. Was this happening or was he dreaming? Did they really want him there?

Eli's eyes were closed, but he beckoned to Rune, now standing sockfooted, watching them with his heart in his throat, as Noemi stroked the hair off his face.

Rune took a shaky breath and eased himself down beside Eli, a few careful inches of room between them. Noemi made a dissatisfied noise and reached across, grabbing Rune's wrist and pulling until he got the message and scooted closer.

Eli sighed, the tension draining from him as Rune pressed close, his wrist still encircled by Noemi's small fingers. She smiled at him over Eli's head and Rune couldn't help the return smile, even as his heart wanted to pound right out of his chest. Eli was solid and warm and fit perfectly against him, his head tipped back and the long, lovely line of his throat exposed. Noemi squeezed Rune's wrist and slid her hand down to tangle her fingers with his.

It wasn't exactly optimal for comfort, especially after a hard game, but Rune would have rather died than move to an actual bed. He fell asleep watching the firelight dancing on Eli's cheekbone and sparking in Noemi's dark eyes.

Noemi

Noemi woke early, slithering out from under Eli's arm in slow stages until she could free herself and tiptoe down the hall to the bathroom. She changed into her running clothes and went to the kitchen to collect Archer.

Rune was already there, bending to talk to him as he clipped the leash on and Archer wriggled happily.

"Oh," Noemi said, and Rune looked up. "I was gonna—"

Rune smiled at her. "You still can. Do you mind if I tag along? I wanted to get a run in."

"Of course not," Noemi said, taking the leash.

They started slow, striking out along the path through the dense trees at an easy pace to give their muscles time to warm up. Noemi focused on her breathing, swinging her arms until her blood was pumping, and then raised an eyebrow at Rune.

"Ready?"

They ran in silence, letting the joy of movement sing through them as they climbed the twisting path toward the peak of the hill that crouched above their house. Noemi wasn't sure if Rune was holding back on her account, but she wasn't having any issues keeping up, her breath free and muscles warm and loose.

The path twined around the hill three times and toward the top, Rune and Noemi slowed in unspoken accord until they were walking when they crested it. Noemi headed for the wrought-iron bench set securely in concrete and began to stretch, unclipping Archer's leash so he could cast about for interesting smells.

Rune followed suit and Noemi watched him out of the corner of her eye. She hadn't been sure, last night, if he'd want to join the cuddle-pile, if it would help him as much as it always helped Eli, but Rune looked better this morning, the shadows lifted from his eyes.

Which made it all the more surprising when he said abruptly, "I think it's time for me to go."

Noemi straightened. "What? You mean like move out?"

Rune avoided her eyes, watching Archer sniffing the base of a tree, and nodded.

"But—" Noemi floundered. "Why?"

That made Rune look up. "What do you mean, why? This was never meant to be a permanent thing, and I've put you out enough, don't you think?"

"But you *haven't*," Noemi protested. She sank to the bench and Rune followed suit, looking cautious. "Is this because of last night? Did we make you uncomfortable? Shit, Rune, I'm—"

"*No*," Rune interrupted. "Last night—" He hesitated, mouth working. "I love you guys, Nomes. I really do. And last night helped so much. Do you do that every time you lose?"

"We try to, yeah." Noemi studied his face intently, looking for clues to how he was feeling. "And we love you too, you know that, right?"

Something eased around Rune's eyes and he almost smiled. "That's good to hear. But I still think I need to go."

"Can you just tell me why?" Noemi asked, scooting nearer. "Why now, why so suddenly? Did something change?"

Rune pinched his mouth shut and folded forward to rest his elbows on his knees, staring down the hill at the city below them. Misery was evident in every line of his body, and Noemi twitched with the urge to comfort him, but she held still, waiting for him to answer.

It took a while but finally he shook his head. "If I tell you, it'll ruin everything. I value your friendship too much. Just… leave it."

"Does that usually work on your friends?" Noemi asked. Rune glanced at her and away again. "Seriously, I want to know. Do you just tell them you have a secret but you're going to shut yourself off and never let any of them in, thanks anyway?"

"That's not what I'm doing," Rune

protested. "I'm trying to *save* us. To keep your friendship."

"By hiding shit from me?" Noemi demanded. "That's not what friends *do*, Rune!"

"I think I'm fucking in love with your husband!" Rune shouted, and Noemi went still. Rune continued, eyes stormy. "Are you happy? Is that what you wanted to hear? I'm trying to do the right fucking thing and get out of here while my heart's still mostly intact, okay? *God*, Nomes, you—" He covered his face with both hands and his shoulders shook briefly.

Noemi somehow remembered how to move and slid across the bench. Rune flinched when she put her arm around him but then he took a ragged breath and slumped against her.

"I'm s-sorry," he whispered thickly.

Noemi rubbed his back. "For what, having good taste?" Distantly, she was impressed her voice was still steady.

Rune just shook his head silently.

"Hey," Noemi said, squeezing him. "Rune, come on. Can you talk to me?"

Rune almost laughed, the noise bitter. "Sure, I'd love to have a discussion with you about how I'm in love with your *husband*. Because there's no possible way that could go wrong."

Noemi sighed, not letting go. "God, boys are so dumb."

"Hey," Rune objected, but there was no heat to it.

"I almost didn't marry Eli," Noemi said, ignoring him.

Rune lifted his head to stare at her. "But —you're perfect together."

"Sure," Noemi agreed. She leaned back against the bench and watched Archer, still tracking interesting scents as Rune straightened to face her. "He's my best friend and I love him more than anything. Getting married just made *sense*, you know? Sharing expenses, being together all the time—plus the idiots on my team somehow started giving me more respect when I put 'Mrs' in front of my name." She shook her head. "Fucking misogyny. But that's beside the point. The *point* is—" She paused, unsure how to say it.

Rune said nothing, watching her intently.

"Look, Eli—I'm not going to speak for him. But for *me*—" She swallowed hard. "I'm not interested in sex. Never really have been. Our marriage—that's not how we work."

Rune's eyes were sharp, but he still didn't speak.

"I felt, going into this—marrying him

—" Noemi continued, "that I wasn't being fair to him. And you want to know something weird?"

Rune raised an eyebrow.

"I thought about the idea of him having sex with someone else, and the idea only bothered me if I didn't know and trust the person to love him and take care of him as much as I do, and if that person understands that I'm always going to be a huge part of Eli's life."

Rune took a careful breath. "What are you saying, Noemi?"

Noemi reached for his hand. "I'm saying you don't have to leave."

Rune shook his head, gripping her hand like it was a life preserver. "You can't mean that. Are you saying Eli—"

"I told you," Noemi interrupted. "I'm not speaking for Eli. I'm speaking for me. And you don't have to leave unless it's truly what you *want*, and not just some idiotic act of nobility. I guess in this much, anyway, I *am* speaking for Eli. He wants you here as much as I do. He told me he does." She squeezed his hand. "Rune."

Rune closed his eyes, still holding on tight.

"Hey," Noemi said gently. "Look at me. Please?"

Rune lifted his head. There were tears in his eyes, and Noemi's heart clenched.

"Oh honey." She pulled him into her arms without thinking about it, and Rune clutched her waist, taking a deep gulp of air. "You got yourself all twisted up thinking I was going to hate you, didn't you?"

Rune nodded against her shoulder and Noemi rubbed his back.

"Are you going to take him away from me?"

"*No*!" Rune twisted away, horror in his eyes. "Why do you think I said I was going to leave? I couldn't—I *wouldn't*, you have to believe me!"

"Okay," Noemi said soothingly. Rune ran a shaking hand through his hair and her heart twisted. "I believe you, Rune, I promise."

"He loves you," Rune said, staring at his feet.

"His heart's big enough to love two people," Noemi said.

"That's not how it works, though."

"Why not?" Archer came panting up and Noemi rubbed his silky ears absently, still watching Rune. "Because society says so? Why are we playing by those rules, anyway? Why aren't we doing what makes *us* happy?"

Rune opened and closed his mouth. "I—"

Noemi patted his knee and stood. "Think about it. And promise me you won't leave until I have a chance to talk to Eli?"

Rune's voice was small when he answered. "I promise."

Noemi grinned at him and bounced on her toes. "Race you back to the house." She was off before Rune could even stand up, Archer delightedly keeping pace.

10

Rune

By the time they made it back, Rune felt a little less like he'd been hollowed out. He tried to squelch the tiny seeds of hope that Noemi's words had planted, but the best he could manage was not to think about it directly. And to not argue with her when she called first shower; they'd learned quickly that two people showering at once was more than the small hot water heater could comfortably handle.

At least, not until he came into the kitchen and saw Eli there, rumpled and relaxed and looking entirely too kissable for Rune's peace of mind.

"Ready for breakfast?" Eli sent a small smile over his shoulder. "Coffee's ready. Better fuel up, we've got the Wolverines tonight."

"Oh god," Rune groaned. He flopped in a chair and put his face on the table. "Does that mean we're playing your brother-in-law and his terrifying boyfriend?"

"Tenny's not terrifying," Eli said, sounding surprised.

"He checked me into the boards the last time I played him," Rune said to the maple-wood. "Never saw it coming. He's intense."

"Intense, sure," Eli said. He set a plate next to Rune's outstretched hand. "But he's really nice. He was at our wedding. I was having some serious jitters and he sat with me, calmed me down. Plus we're having dinner at Coach's after the game."

Rune lifted his head. "That'll be nice." He tugged the plate closer. "Maybe I'll go out while you're gone."

"Well, you can," Eli said, seating himself opposite. "But you're also invited."

Rune froze. "To dinner."

"Mhmm." Eli took a bite of eggs and made a pleased noise.

"To dinner with… Coach and his entire family."

"Yep." Eli took another bite. His bearing was loose, smile lingering in his eyes, and Rune scrutinized him.

"Seriously, how are you in such a good mood?"

"I'm always in a good mood," Eli said,

completely straight-faced, and didn't crack until Rune laughed, grinning bright and open back at him. "Like I said yesterday, Noemi and I talked some stuff out. I guess I didn't realize how much it was bugging me, but now it's—better."

What did that mean? Rune couldn't ask, no matter how much he wanted to. He picked up his fork and took a bite.

"Anyway yeah, Coach told me to tell you they'd love for you to be there."

Rune couldn't remember the last time he'd been invited to a coach's house for dinner, but then again, he'd never lived with the coach's daughter and son-in-law before. If he stayed—part of him still couldn't believe he was considering it—it was likely something that would happen again.

Besides, it was probably a bad idea to turn down an invitation from someone who was effectively your boss. At least, that was what Rune told himself, even though he couldn't imagine Coach Caron being the kind of person to hold it against him.

"If you're sure I won't be intruding?"

Eli actually laughed at that, using his fork to pull the last of his eggs into a pile at the center of his plate. "Please. I know you haven't been here that long, but Coach and his wife love having people over. I think they miss when Adam and his friends were in and out of the house all the time."

Before Rune could come up with another excuse, or talk himself out of it, Eli took his last bite and pushed back from the table. "I'm gonna go say hi to Nomes before she has to go to work, but for real, everyone would love to have you. Maybe you and Tenny could even make friends."

And then he disappeared, leaving Rune to eat the rest of his breakfast without tasting a thing, trying not to think about anything.

Eli

When Eli opened the bedroom door, Noemi was just coming out of the bathroom, a towel wrapped around her body.

It was amazing how much lighter he felt, not wondering if he was supposed to perform an attraction he didn't feel. Just knowing Noemi would hate for him to pretend to feel something he didn't made his smile extra wide when she looked up and saw him.

"Good run?"

She smiled back as she crossed to the closet. "Yeah, I needed to get out, and

Rune's good company. Can you let him know he's good to shower?"

Eli leaned back out into the hallway. "Rune, shower's all yours!" He waited until he heard a muted shout of assent before closing the door to give Noemi privacy.

"He's a lot taller than you." Eli couldn't resist the chirp. "Sure he didn't leave you in the dust?"

Noemi sniffed, pulling clothes out and tossing them on the bed. "Unlike *some* people, Rune is a gentleman. He would never. Something perhaps you could stand to learn from him."

Eli conceded the point with a tilt of the head. "Looking forward to dinner?"

"Yeah, it's gonna be so good to see Adam and Tenny again." Her voice was briefly muffled as her head disappeared into a shirt. "After you kick their asses, obviously."

"Obviously." He couldn't help smiling at her, relief and ease bubbling up inside of him. "And Rune said he'd come to dinner, so they can meet him."

Noemi's smile matched his, warm and happy and open. "Oh, perfect."

He sat on the edge of the bed, basking in the comfortable silence as she joined him to put on her socks and shoes.

"Speaking of Rune."

The comment was so sudden and unexpected that he blinked for a few seconds, trying to figure it out. "Were we?"

"We were." Stepping over to the dresser, Noemi started putting her hair up, her eyes meeting his in the mirror. "Have you ever noticed how hot he is?"

The comment had heat rising in Eli's cheeks. "It's not polite to notice things like that about your guests. Not to mention a teammate."

From the look Noemi's reflection gave him, she wasn't going to let him get away with being deliberately obtuse. "Not only is he hot, he's also really nice, and sweet. And smart, holy shit."

"What exactly are you getting at here?"

"I think you know." Noemi deliberated over earrings before choosing a pair of pearl studs and turning back around.

"I'm pretty sure I don't, or I'd better not, because if you're suggesting I date Rune—"

Noemi arched her eyebrows at him. "Why not?"

"He thinks we're married," Eli pointed out.

That earned him a gentle—for Noemi—punch in the arm. "We *are* married, jackass. And I love you, which means I want you to be happy. You like Rune."

Eli sputtered. "Of course I like Rune. He's a good friend."

Noemi opened her mouth and her alarm went off. Eli cast a quick, grateful glance heavenward as Noemi grabbed her phone.

"Shit. I'm gonna be late." She kissed Eli on the cheek. "I'll see you after the game. This conversation isn't over. I love you."

"Love you too." Eli got the answer out on reflex, the world still tilting under his feet.

He had no idea how long he sat on the side of the bed, turning Noemi's words over in his head. She thought he and Rune—*he and Rune*—were a good idea. His *wife* wanted him to date *Rune*. How was this his life? He couldn't help the incredulous laugh, staring at the wall as if he'd find the answers there.

No answers had appeared by the time they needed to leave, but hockey schedules didn't stop for personal crises. Eli gathered his gear and did his best to act normal as he and Rune drove to the arena.

Of course Rune noticed. Not only was he hot and sweet and smart, he was also thoughtful and considerate, damn him. And observant.

"Everything okay?" he asked as Eli pulled into player parking.

The wave of affection threatened to

swamp Eli, but he forced himself to put it away. Not for long, but for now. They had practice, and then a game to win. Time enough for him to think about this afterward.

"Yeah, I'm good." The smile he gave Rune was real, and Rune's shoulders eased as he smiled back.

"Good." Rune opened his door, waiting for Eli to circle around before he started walking. "Let's kick some ass."

11

Eli

Noemi pushed through the front door into her parents' familiar wide hall. She took a deep breath and sent Eli a quick smile over her shoulder.

"Smells like home," she said, and unclipped Archer's leash so he could dash through to the kitchen ahead of them. "We're here!" she shouted.

"Kitchen!" Colette called in response.

Rune and Eli trailed after Noemi—like a pair of slightly awkward ducklings, Eli thought wryly—as she led the way down the hall past the circular staircase and into the kitchen, where Noemi was promptly swept off her feet by Adam, who pounced when she stepped through the door and spun her in a circle as she shrieked and slapped at him.

"Let me *go*, you asshole, or I'll get Tenny to put itching powder in your jock!"

Adam snorted, setting her back on her feet. "Tenny likes me better than you."

"I wouldn't count on it," Etienne put in from where he stood next to their mother, watching with an amused grin. "She's nicer. And I bet she's willing to bribe me." He nodded at Eli, who shared his smile.

Adam clutched his chest dramatically. "Betrayed by my sister *and* my boyfriend!"

Laughing, Colette rolled her eyes. "Behave, children. Eli's used to you, but we don't want to scare Rune off."

"I'm a hockey player." Rune was grinning, too. "I don't scare that easily."

"Still, you're a guest." Colette extended her hand. "I'm Colette, and these two monsters are my offspring, supposedly. I promise I really did try to teach them how to behave."

Accepting the hand, Rune smiled back at her. "Thank you so much for inviting me, Mrs. Caron. Your house is lovely and so is your family."

"Colette." She smiled at him, dark blue eyes warm. "And thank you. William's just getting changed and then we'll eat. Can I get you something to drink?"

They ate in the family dining room, Rune on one side of Eli and Noemi on the other.

"So, Rune," Colette said as she handed the mashed potatoes around. "Tell us about yourself."

Rune obeyed, regaling them with stories about the youth league in Germany. His eyes were bright, posture loose, and Eli wanted desperately to kiss him. Rune glanced at him and his lips curved. Eli smiled back and took Noemi's hand.

Etienne was watching him when Eli glanced up. One eyebrow twitched up just slightly but he said nothing.

After dinner, Adam grabbed Noemi's arm. "We'll clean up, Mom."

Noemi protested, but Adam dragged her toward the kitchen without listening.

"I don't trust it," Coach said, looking wary.

"Don't *question* it," Colette said, shooing everyone else toward the den. "I don't care *why* they're doing it as long as they do."

Noemi

Noemi waited until they got to the

kitchen before twisting out of Adam's grip. "What the fuck?"

"I just wanted a chance to talk to you." He was still smiling, but his forehead was furrowed. "See how married life was treating you."

"It's good," Noemi said slowly. "Some adjustments, but overall we're doing really well."

For some reason, Adam looked even more pained. "And, uh, the thing you, uh—"

She was tempted to see how long it took him to get to the point, but Rune and Eli were at the mercy of her parents and she didn't feel like seeing how long it took one of them to crack. "I was being an idiot about it, but we finally talked, and it was good."

"Good." Adam let out a long breath. "I don't have to kill him."

Noemi flung her arms around his neck. Maybe a little harder than she'd planned, but Adam caught her, grunting softly. "I love you."

"Love you too." He squeezed her gently.

Noemi let him go and turned to open the dishwasher. "So, how are you and Tenny?"

Adam sighed. "He's so great, Nomes.

Like seriously, I don't know how I got so lucky."

"Yeah?"

They filled the dishwasher as Adam talked, collapsing against the counter in a fit of helpless giggles as he tried to tell her a story involving Etienne and the mascot of the Wolverines.

"God, you should have seen his *face*." Adam wiped away tears of laughter and put a plate in the rack.

"When are you going to propose?" Noemi teased.

Adam froze. "Uh."

"Wait, seriously? Have you already? Adam Alexis Noah Caron, if you're engaged and you haven't told us—"

Adam waved his hands frantically until she shut up and glared at him.

"Well?"

"I *haven't* yet," Adam hissed, casting a furtive glance at the door like Etienne might be lurking behind it. "But I, uh… might have bought a ring?"

Noemi shrieked with joy and threw her arms around his neck again and Adam caught her, his laugh vibrating through him.

"Fuck, I'm so freaked out, Nomes," he said when he set her back on her feet. "What if he says no?"

Noemi gave him a look of withering

derision. "Are we talking about the same guy here? The one who's clearly, obviously, *disgustingly* in love with you? You really think he'd say no?"

"I just—" Adam shifted his weight, looking unsure. "I mean, he was there during the whole… you know."

"Going blind?" Noemi said helpfully.

Adam glared at her. "Thank you, yes. I know he loves me, but I'm just worried. What if we get split up? Traded to different teams?"

"If you do, you'll deal with it," Noemi said. "C'mon, Adam, you grew up in a hockey family, you know what it's like. Tenny knows what it's like too. Long distance sucks, but you can make it work, if you really want to." She clutched her face, suddenly overwhelmed. "Oh my god, my big brother's getting *married*!"

Adam shushed her again but he couldn't stop his grin. "I think I might be, yeah."

Eli

Toward the end of the evening, Eli found a moment to slip away. Noemi was deep in conversation with her mother, Adam was talking to Rune, and Etienne was being grilled by Coach about something.

With no one looking at him, Eli took the opportunity to step out onto the back porch. William and Colette's property was set into a hill, the bay glittering cold silver in the moonlight at its feet. Eli leaned his elbows on the railing and gazed out over the water.

Despite everything, all the uncertainty and exhaustion because of the constant struggle to deny his true self, he felt more at peace than he had in a very long time. He had Noemi. He had the team. And maybe—

The door slid open and Eli turned to see Etienne stepping outside.

"Hey," he said. "Do you mind if I join you?"

"Of course not." Eli straightened as Etienne joined him. "You played a great game tonight."

Etienne slanted a smile at him, eyes gleaming in the moonlight, and leaned on the railing beside him. "So did you. And Rune."

Eli shrugged. "We got lucky. Next time it'll be yours."

Etienne conceded that with a tilt of his head and they stood in companionable silence for a few minutes.

"I love this family," Etienne said after a minute. "But they can be… a lot."

That startled Eli into a laugh. "You're not wrong. But they're great."

"Oh, for sure." Etienne turned his head and scrutinized for a minute. "You look… happier than the last time we talked."

Before the wedding. When Eli's options had been making a run for it or living a lie.

Eli rubbed the back of his neck. "I —yeah."

"Figured some stuff out?"

"You could say that."

Etienne just nodded, but Eli looked at him for a minute.

"You know, don't you?"

Etienne straightened. "I don't know anything unless you tell me personally. It's not my place to speculate."

"But you suspect." Eli couldn't have said why he was pushing. Maybe because the thought of someone—someone other than his dearest friends—knowing his secret somehow made it feel more real, more like something that could actually… happen.

"It's not for me to say," Etienne said quietly.

"You never even told Adam, did you?" Eli asked. The surprise in Etienne's eyes told him the answer. "Jesus, you really are a great guy."

Etienne shifted his feet. "I'm really not."

"I'm gay," Eli said.

The words fell into silence. Eli held his breath, counting to ten.

Ten, nine, eight….

At four, Etienne spoke.

"Okay." There was absolutely no emotion on his face.

Eli laughed. He couldn't help it. He wrapped his arms around his ribs and laughed until Etienne took a step forward, clearly alarmed, and Eli had to lift a hand to reassure him.

"I'm fine," he managed through the giggles. "Do you—oh God, I needed that—do you realize that's the first time I've said the words out loud?"

"I had a hunch, from your reaction," Etienne said. His lips were twitching. "How's it feel?"

"Good," Eli said, surprised to find it was true. "Really good. Better."

"Does Noemi know?" Etienne's tone was carefully neutral, but Eli sobered immediately.

"Yeah." Something in Etienne's posture eased like he'd been afraid of the wrong answer, but Eli didn't pause to let him speak. "I tried—I really tried to be right for her. To be *attracted* to her. You know?"

"Not really, but keep going," Etienne said.

"I just wanted…." Eli blew out a breath.

"I wanted her to be happy, and *I* wanted to be happy, and we're happy together, so I thought… marriage made sense. She's my best friend and I love being with her. I told myself the attraction would follow."

"Not how it works, in my experience," Etienne said dryly. "But you said she knows?"

"I love her so much," Eli said. "She's trying to set me up with someone."

Etienne's eyebrows winged upward. "Wow. That's—wow."

"I know." Eli half-laughed, rubbing his face. "I don't deserve her." He glanced up. "You won't… tell anyone, right? Sorry, stupid question. Of course you won't tell anyone."

"I'm glad things are better," Etienne said instead of answering. "If you ever need someone to talk to, I'm—well, I'm not great with words, but I can listen anytime."

Eli put a hand out and Etienne took it. "Thank you," Eli said. "We should probably go back before they come looking for us."

THEY RODE home in comfortable silence, everyone worn out from the long day. Rune wished them a good night and pecked

Noemi on the cheek, giving Eli a soft smile before disappearing into his room.

As Eli and Noemi got ready for bed, he could feel her watching him. At first he ignored it, but finally he gave up with a sigh.

"Out with it."

"Have you given any more thought to what we discussed earlier?" Noemi asked, flipping the covers back so she could slide into the bed.

"Absolutely not," Eli said immediately. He rinsed his toothbrush and set it back in its holder before joining her in the bed. "I don't even know what you're referring to."

Noemi poked him in the ribs, making him yelp. "Funny man. You know exactly what I'm talking about."

Eli scooted down to lie on his side and Noemi followed suit, watching his face carefully. Eli sighed. "Nomes, you can't seriously mean it."

"I seriously can," Noemi retorted. "He's perfect for you and you know it."

"Perfect or not, I'm a deeply closeted married man with no plans to divorce or come out any time soon. I'm—I can't. I can't risk everything just to… get my rocks off. He's *team*, Nomes. What if things go wrong?" He shook his head. "I can't do it."

"Then he's moving out," Noemi said, her voice even.

Eli sat up straight. "He what?"

"He told me this morning. He's leaving."

"No." Eli shook his head again. "He can't. He can't, Nomes. He—he *belongs* here."

Noemi arched a brow silently.

"Fuck." Eli collapsed back onto the pillows, turmoil churning in his stomach. "What did he say? When he told you? Why is he leaving?"

"I can't tell you," Noemi said gently. "At least not yet. But that's why you need to talk to him. If you have that strong a reaction to the thought of him leaving, can you really live with yourself if you *don't* say anything?"

"I just…." Eli rolled onto his back to stare at the ceiling. "Do you have any idea how *weird* this feels? That my *wife* is trying to talk me into dating someone else?"

Noemi patted his arm. "That's because you've bought into society's norms, honey. You gotta shake that shit off. Do what makes *you* happy."

"And you," Eli said, turning his head on the pillow to meet her eyes. "I want to do what makes *you* happy."

Noemi arched a brow. "You need to hear it? Fine. Eli, it would make me the happiest woman in the world if you were to ask our roommate on a date. And hopefully kiss him within an inch of his life after dessert."

Eli laughed under his breath, dragging his hands down his face. "I can't believe this. It feels like a dream. What do you want me to even *say*?"

"Something suave and cool," Noemi suggested.

"Have you *met* me?" Eli retorted, and Noemi laughed.

"Something honest, then."

Something honest.

Long after Noemi fell asleep, Eli lay awake, still staring at the ceiling. He'd expected to feel more guilt at the idea of kissing someone else, but instead there was a swirling maelstrom of confusion, terror, and excitement. *It isn't just any random person, anyway,* he thought, listening to Noemi's steady breathing beside him. *It's Rune. Who fights for me, makes me laugh,* gets *me.* The thought of Rune holding him made Eli dizzy with hunger. The fact that Noemi *wanted* that for him made his heart ache with how much he loved her.

Giving up on the idea of sleep, he slid

quietly out of bed and padded down the hall to the kitchen for a glass of milk.

He froze in the doorway at the sight of Rune's broad shoulders, backlit by the light from the refrigerator.

Rune glanced up and smiled, milk in hand. "Couldn't sleep either?" His hair was rumpled, falling in his face, and he looked entirely too kissable for Eli's peace of mind.

"Good thing we have tomorrow off," Eli said, proud of himself for keeping his voice steady.

Rune added more milk to the pot and stirred as Eli sat down at the table and watched him. Now that he was giving himself permission to look, *really* look, there was so much to appreciate about Rune physically. From the way his broad shoulders stretched the fabric of his T-shirt, the planes of his shoulder blades clearly visible against the weave, to the way his ass filled out his soft flannel pants in a graceful curve, he was pure, mouthwatering perfection.

Something honest.

Eli had no idea what to say. How did he even open the conversation?

Rune poured the milk into mugs and set one in front of Eli before settling opposite him. The light over the stove was the only illumination in the room, and it haloed him in a faint golden glow as he took a sip.

"Noemi's family likes you," Eli said after a few minutes.

Rune's mouth curved. "That's a relief. Dinner was nice."

"I came out to Tenny," Eli said abruptly, and snapped his mouth shut. *How's that for honest?* Terror made his heart bang against his ribcage violently. He set the mug down and put his hands in his lap so Rune wouldn't see how they were shaking.

Rune had gone very still. "Did you just say—"

"Yes," Eli said.

"You mean as in—"

"Yes," Eli repeated.

Rune stared at him. His face was unreadable, eyes hooded and intent in the dim room. "You're saying you're—"

"I'm gay," Eli interrupted. He clutched the seat of his chair to keep himself upright.

Rune sat back in his chair. He rubbed his mouth, expression still impossible to decipher. Eli squirmed.

"Can you… maybe say something?" he finally asked, hating the pleading note in his voice.

"Sorry, I'm… processing," Rune said. He hadn't looked away from Eli yet. "Is he the first person you told?"

Eli shook his head. "Dav's known since Juniors. And I told Noemi a few days ago."

Rune's eyebrows lifted. "Is that what you talked about?"

"Among other things," Eli said.

"Huh." Rune let silence lapse again and Eli waited, pulling on his meditation exercises to keep himself from vibrating right out of his skin. "What did Noemi think?" Rune asked, then waved it off. "Not my business." He looked up again. "Actually, I still want to know."

Eli's laugh was mostly nerves, thin and stretched to breaking. He rubbed his palms on his sweats. "She wanted to—to set me up with someone." *You.* He didn't say it.

Rune nodded slowly. "She's amazing."

"I know."

"Do you think you'll take her up on it?"

Eli fidgeted. "I don't… know. It's all so new, you know? But I think—maybe. At some point, when it's sunk in." *When I can figure out how to ask you.*

Rune nodded and stood, making Eli blink. "I should sleep. Thank you, um… for telling me. Trusting me. I'll see you in the morning." He set his mug in the sink and strode from the room before Eli could think of anything to say.

Eli sat in the silent kitchen for a minute as his milk grew cold. That was it then, was it? Rune clearly wasn't interested. Whatever

Noemi had thought, she'd been off the mark.

He wanted to curl around the hurt, let it bloom between his ribs, but there was anger growing at the same time.

"No," he said aloud to the empty room. *No.* Rune had asked him out before he'd known he was married. He'd been *interested* in him and shown it clearly. It hadn't just been Eli's wishful thinking. There'd been *something* there.

Eli stood, clenching his fists. He couldn't just... let it go like that. He had to *know.*

His feet carried him out of the kitchen and down the hall. Rune's door was closed but Eli could hear movement inside.

He knocked.

Waited.

Knocked again.

It was over a minute before Rune opened the door. His eyes were hooded, watchful in the dark hall.

"You're sleeping in Noemi's room," Eli said without preamble.

Rune's eyes widened but he said nothing, pushing the door wider.

"When Jay volunteered us, she got all her stuff out of here and moved it back in with me," Eli forged on. "We didn't want you to know—to think—" He took a shaky breath. "I love her so much but we—we don't—"

Rune was still silent, letting Eli fumble through without help, but something around his eyes had softened as he watched him.

"Don't go," Eli said. Pleaded. "Nomes said you were moving out. Rune, I—"

Rune let go of the door and took a quick step forward. Eli swallowed hard. Rune was gazing down at him, eyes unreadable, but they were toe-to-toe, Rune so close Eli could feel his body heat through his thin T-shirt.

Slowly, giving Eli plenty of time to react, Rune lifted a hand. Eli held his breath, eyes slipping shut. When Rune cupped his face, it felt like a benediction, an absolving of Eli's sins. Tears pricked his eyelids and he swayed into Rune's heat.

"Rune," he whispered, and his voice failed him.

"Shh," Rune said. He tipped Eli's head up and their lips met as the first tear slid scalding hot down Eli's cheek.

Rune's mouth was soft and sweet, asking but not demanding. His tongue caressed the seam of Eli's lips and Eli caught his breath and opened to him, falling into his heat with a helpless noise. Rune wrapped his arms around Eli's waist and pulled him closer, muscling him back against the wall so Eli was caged in, safe and protected from the world. His world *was* Rune, deepening the kiss now, his breathing uneven, and it helped, somehow, helped to know Rune was as undone by this as Eli was, gave Eli the courage to go up on tiptoe and snake his arms around Rune's neck, plastering himself against him.

The tears were still falling when they broke for air, and Rune pressed their foreheads together, wiping Eli's cheek with the pad of his thumb.

"Don't cry," he murmured, voice rough.

Eli shook his head wordlessly, tightening his grip. He wasn't sure how to explain that they were happy tears, that his heart was so full he thought it might crack open and fill the hall with light and blind them both.

"Will you stay?" he managed.

Rune's laugh was unsteady. "What do you think?" he whispered, and then he was lowering his head to find Eli's mouth again and Eli couldn't help his hiccuping laugh as he kissed him back, wet and messy and full of all the things he didn't know how to say yet. For the first time in his life, he felt like maybe, just maybe, he'd find the words someday soon.

EPILOGUE

Two months later

Rune

Rune jogged up the steps to the house, sweat slicking his skin and plastering his shirt to his back. Inside, he grabbed the hem and hauled it off over his head, shaking sweaty hair out of his eyes and dropping the shirt in the hamper on his way through the laundry room into the kitchen.

"I'm home," he announced unnecessarily to the occupants of the kitchen—Noemi at the sink washing dishes and Eli at the table, reading something on his phone.

Noemi curled her lip. "You're disgusting, is what you are. Go shower."

"Too good for a little honest sweat?" Rune teased, and lunged. Noemi's shriek was blood-curdling but it was too late, he had her in his arms, spinning her in circles around the room as she flailed and smacked wildly at him.

When he set her back on her feet, they were both breathless with giggles. Noemi punched his arm one final time for good measure and Rune yelped, grinning at Eli, laughing at them from his seat.

"She's mean," he commented, and rounded the table to bend and give him a kiss.

Eli huffed amusement against Rune's mouth. "You're a horrible person," he told him.

"You're into it, though," Rune countered. He winked as Eli sputtered and sauntered from the room, still grinning.

It had been two months of taking it slow. Rune knew Eli wanted it—him—as badly as Rune did, but they were both determined to do it right. That meant soft kisses outside bedroom doors or traded on the couch, hands never straying below the waist. It meant lingering glances, teasing flashes of skin, and—at least in Rune's case—a whole lot of jerking off.

As much as he dreamed of taking Eli apart, he wasn't going to rush into anything.

The moment had to be right. Neither one of them felt comfortable having their first time in a hotel room, or in the house with Noemi there, no matter how many times she complained about the sexual tension and ordered them to get a room or offered to go to Juliet's.

Rune turned on the shower and dropped his shorts on the floor. Noemi was leaving for work within the hour and they had to leave for the rink not long after. Plenty of time for a leisurely jerk-off session thinking about Eli's mouth and those lovely, clever hands.

When he got out of the shower, pleasantly drained and skin still tingling from the remnants of his orgasm, Eli was sitting on his bed, feet crossed neatly at the ankles.

Rune stopped dead and clutched the towel around his waist.

"Seen it," Eli reminded him, lips twitching.

"This is different," Rune said, holding the towel tighter. "What are you doing here?"

"Appreciating the view?" Eli suggested. His smile widened and he stood to cross the room, stopping a foot away.

Rune gulped. "E…."

"Relax, I'm not going to ravish you with Noemi down the hall," Eli said. He raked his gaze over Rune's half-naked body. "Much as I want to."

"You're *killing* me," Rune groaned. "Can I just—" He reached out with one hand, the other holding the towel in place, and reeled him in.

He could never get enough of kissing Eli. There was a sort of stunned, wondrous delight in the way Eli responded to him, like he'd never expected or imagined this happening and he was afraid of waking up. Rune sank his hand into the silky strands of Eli's hair, cupping his head and deepening the kiss until Eli was clinging to him, breath sharp and ragged.

Rune broke the kiss and mouthed along Eli's jaw, nipping and sucking lightly as Eli swayed.

"Fuck," he moaned, tucking his face into Rune's throat. "I had a reason for—I can't *think* when you're d-doing that—"

Rune took pity on him and lifted his head. Eli stayed pressed against him a minute longer, but finally he stirred and took a reluctant step back. Rune smiled down at him.

"Hey," he murmured. "I love you."

Eli's smile was like the dawn breaking. "I

love you too," he said. "I wanted to tell you —Noemi just got word she's going on the next roadie with the boys. Tonight. She'll be gone until day after tomorrow. And she said to tell you if we don't do something with the time, she's never speaking to either of us again."

"Is that so?" Rune said, smile widening. "I'm sure I can think of something to do."

Eli blushed, ducking his head to hide his own smile. "I should go get ready."

Rune let him go regretfully, watching as he slipped out the door before turning to find clothes.

Part of him couldn't really believe where he was, in a relationship with a married man whose wife had given them her enthusiastic blessing. It was one of the first things Eli had managed to say, once the kissing and the wiping of tears was past and they were in the living room, sitting on the couch facing each other.

"I don't want a divorce," he'd said, and braced himself as if for a blow. "If—if you don't—I understand if you—"

"Shut up," Rune said gently. He squeezed Eli's hands. "Talk it out, let me hear it."

Eli squared his shoulders. "I love Noemi." He smiled almost ruefully. "I say that so much but it's true. I don't… I've never wanted to have sex with her, even when I tried to tell myself I did. But she's literally the best person I've ever met. She's like… an extension of me. I can't imagine life without her. So I don't—if you want me, y-you have to accept that we're a package deal. Because I w-won't let her go just because you get jealous or something."

Rune just nodded. "I would honestly think less of you if you did," he admitted. "Noemi's incredible and I would never want you to cut her out of your life."

"Really?" The hope on Eli's face was almost heartbreaking.

"Really," Rune said. He leaned forward and brushed a light kiss across Eli's mouth, mostly because he could. "Maybe it's not a traditional relationship, but who gives a fuck? The main thing is that we're all happy. Which—are you *sure* she's—"

"She's been pushing me at you for weeks," Eli said, laughing softly. "She knows how good you are for me. And maybe… I'm good for you?"

Rune hauled him into a much more aggressive kiss at that. "You are so good for me," he said between kisses. "God, E, I never thought this could work. I tried to leave, did Nomes tell you?"

Eli settled back on the couch, still holding Rune's hand, and nodded. "She didn't say why, just that you were thinking of going."

"It's because I thought I'd fallen in love with a married man who couldn't love me back," Rune said, and Eli's mouth fell open.

"You—"

"Against my better judgment," Rune said softly. "I didn't mean to, you're just… ugh." Eli's smile was his favorite thing, he thought, the way it lit his solemn gray eyes and made the dimple in his cheek flash. He couldn't help leaning forward to kiss him again. "But yeah, she made me agree to stay until she talked to you. She's amazing, Eli. If you fuck that up, *I'll* never forgive you."

Eli laughed outright and opened his mouth to say something.

"Oh my God," Noemi said from the doorway, and they both spun. She had both hands over her mouth, tears spilling down her cheeks. "Did it happen? Did you guys *finally* figure your shit out?"

Eli scrambled off the couch and reached for her. "I kissed him, Nomes," he managed, and Noemi flung her arms around him.

"Oh, my boys, my darling boys," she said through her tears, and reached for

Rune, hauling him into the hug. "You're both so stupid and I love you *so much.*"

Eli laughed and met Rune's eyes over her head. They shared a private smile and Eli kissed the crown of Noemi's head.

Rune held on tight, the happiness within him threatening to lift his feet right off the ground. Never in his life had he imagined this was how things would work out, but it was *better*, somehow, standing there in both Noemi's and Eli's arms, surrounded and sheltered in their love.

"ARE YOU COMING?" Eli shouted from the hall, and Rune shook himself.

"Almost ready!" he called back, and scrambled into his clothes.

ACKNOWLEDGMENTS

Thank you to everyone who helped make this book a reality. Specifically, Aaliya and Sarah for brainstorming plot points and really bringing the characters to life, Sarah for pushing me through the bits where I got stuck, and CJ for reading everything and begging for more. You guys keep me going and I'm so grateful for you.

ABOUT THE AUTHOR

Michaela Grey told stories to put herself to sleep since she was old enough to hold a conversation in her head. When she learned to write, she began putting those stories down on paper. She resides in the Texas Hill Country with her cats, and is perpetually on the hunt for peaceful writing time.

When she's not writing, she's watching hockey or blogging about writing and men on knife shoes chasing a frozen Oreo around the ice while trying to keep her cat off the keyboard.

Tumblr: greymichaela.tumblr.com
Twitter: @GreyMichaela
Facebook: www.facebook.com/Grey-Michaela
E-mail: greymichaela@gmail.com

Want to find out when her next book comes out? Sign up for her newsletter here or follow her on Amazon here

ALSO BY MICHAELA GREY

Beloved Scars

Broken Halo

Broken Rules

Broken Trust

Broken Promises

Blindside Hit:

A Toronto Wolverines Novel

ABOUT THE AUTHOR

Ariel Bishop is an American romance and erotica author who feels strongly that all love triangles are best resolved through healthy polyamory. She lives in the Ozarks with her partners, their children and two bunnies that rejoice in the names Reginald von Pancakes and Snickers.

More information about her books can be found at her website where you can sign up for her mailing list. You can also find her on Tumblr, Twitter, and Facebook. For sneak previews of upcoming books in the Tripping series and other rewards, you can support her on Patreon

Keep reading for a list of her other works and a sneak peek at book 5 in the Tripping series, Blue Line.

BLUE LINE SNEAK PEEK

THE CALL COMES on an off day, at least.

To be honest, Seth has been waiting for this for awhile now. He's been having a blast with the Abs, playing actual CHL games. But he was only called up in the first place because Mikey got injured, because Tolly needed a new D-partner.

Ever since Mikey came back, Seth has been expecting the call. The *Thanks for what you've given us, but—*. The *you're a good player, son, but the salary cap—*. The *you're playing strong out there, I'm sure we'll see you up here in no time.*

When the call comes, though, it isn't the one he's expecting.

"Say that again?"

His agent sounds simultaneously harried and amused, which is pretty par for the course with Devi; he's never heard her sound any different. "They traded you to the Thunderbirds, kid. Pack your bags."

Seth has no idea what he says for the rest of the conversation. The words must make sense, because Devi doesn't call him on not paying attention. Of course, he is paying attention. He could repeat back her side of the conversation verbatim.

He's just also processing.

When the call ends, he sits there, staring around at the short-term rental the team had found him. He'd never bothered to really settle in; he's always known his presence here was temporary. But even if he didn't personalize his surroundings, he hadn't realized how much he was expecting to go back to Calgary, to still have the option of spending time in Edmonton sometimes, until that option was gone.

Before he could stew too long, the phone rings again. He's surprised to see Cisco's name on the screen, then surprised at himself for being surprised. Of course someone would have told Cisco, and of course Cisco would call him.

"Hey, man, I just heard." Cisco doesn't bother trying to sound overly cheerful. Seth appreciates that.

"Yeah, well, that makes two of us."

Something rustles in the background of

the call, maybe Cisco, maybe Leo. "When do they want you down there?"

"They're actually on a roadie right now, so I'm supposed to fly out tonight and meet them in Boise after they play."

"Yeah? Okay, so we're taking you out to dinner."

Seth finds himself grinning. "Do I get a choice?"

"No, you don't get a choice. I'll text you the restaurant and the time."

"They should give you one of the As, if you're gonna boss people around for free." Seth can't keep the fondness out of his voice. "I'm gonna miss you, Sunshine."

There's a smile in Cisco's voice when he says, "Yeah, me too. See you in a bit."

The call ends, but an answering smile stretches Seth's face as he gets up to look for clothes. No matter where Cisco has in mind, he probably should be wearing something nicer than a UMinn t-shirt long past its prime and a pair of sweatpants he hasn't washed in at least a week. Maybe two.

Instead of getting a text directly from Cisco, it comes in through the team group text. Seth shakes his head, but he can't deny the warm feeling in his chest at the number of replies, at how many members of the team are dropping plans and rearranging schedules to come say goodbye.

Once he's dressed, he has a few minutes before he needs to leave for the restaurant, so he pulls up video from the Thunderbirds' last game. One minute in, he can't control the wince at what he's seeing. Like, he knows the Abs have one of the strongest d-corps in the league, but watching the Thunderbirds d-men completely fail, over and over again, to do their job, is just painful.

He gets so caught up, between the video and texts from Harri, one of the Thunderbird's As, that he loses track of time, enough that he has to rush a little to not be late to his own goodbye dinner. But even as he's weaving through traffic, he's feeling a little more settled, a little better about the whole thing.

Maybe they actually need him.

Preorder Blue Line now!

www.ingramcontent.com/pod-product-compliance
Ingram Content Group UK Ltd.
Pitfield, Milton Keynes, MK11 3LW, UK
UKHW020417250726
13967UKWH00007B/2684